Charity Child

SARA SEALE

Originally published as Harlequin Romance #991

HARLEQUIN
CLASSIC LIBRARY

TORONTO • NEW YORK • LOS ANGELES • LONDON
AMSTERDAM • PARIS • SYDNEY • HAMBURG
STOCKHOLM • ATHENS • TOKYO • MILAN

Original hardcover edition published by
Mills & Boon Limited 1959
ISBN 0-373-80122-X

Harlequin edition first published February 1966
Harlequin Classic Library edition published March 1983

Printed in Canada

CHAPTER ONE

"BUT, MY dear aunt, your reasoning is preposterous!"

Mrs. Clara Stubbs, who preferred to be known as Astrea, the name which had enjoyed brief fame in the musical world nearly forty years ago, turned to regard her nephew with a speculative eye. When he addressed her as aunt she knew she had outraged the logical conclusions of his legal mind.

"I'm a preposterous woman, as you've often pointed out," she replied mildly.

Marc Gentle's lean, forensic face softened in a reluctant smile. None knew better than he that his aunt's mildness was deceptive. She gloried in her eccentricity and was always prepared to do battle with him.

"Now listen to me," he said patiently. "This girl is a complete stranger to you, like all the others, only this one you find thumping the piano in some scruffy little music shop in the Charing Cross Road. That and the fact that she was born under the sign of Aquarius constitute your sole arguments for employing her as a companion. I put it to you, is that sound reasoning?"

"Don't address me as if I were in the witness-box," she said crossly. "And she did not thump the piano; her touch was very light and delicate, and the influence of Aquarius is most important. Don't you know that these subjects show a strong tendency to form solidly helpful habits?"

"Very likely," he returned dryly, "but the fact remains you know nothing whatever about the girl and she quite obviously took advantage of your—er—eccentricity."

"Not at all. I lost her her job."

"By making a scene in the shop."

"And why not, pray? They were very rude to me. They had never heard of Astrea. One assistant even alluded to me as an old bag. I was not intended to hear, of course, but my ears are still sharp."

In the small silence that fell between them he regarded her with a moment's compassionate understanding. Astrea was a big woman with the sagging diaphragm muscles of the opera singer gone to seed, and her large bust was hung about with chains and necklaces from which dangled jewelled charms of the Signs of the Zodiac, which she was never without. She was said to be in her late sixties, but was probably older, and favored clothes of no known period, with many floating scarves and draperies, but she still dyed her hair a rich Titian and her once fine eyes were always heavily mascaraed. She must often, he supposed, present a figure of fun to the present generation which had never heard of her, and her insistence that the magic of her once-famous name could never quite die was, perhaps, a little pathetic.

"I'm sorry they were rude to you," he said gently. "Another generation forgets easily, you know, and this was, after all, a cheap little publishing firm dependent on the latest jive for their sales."

"But this girl remembered," she said imperiously. "She knew my records. It was in my defence that she crossed swords with the manager and lost her job, so you see—"

She left the sentence unfinished and he sighed impatiently and turned away to the long, uncurtained window which gave on to an uninterrupted view of the Sussex downs lying calm and sparkling in the frost and moonlight. Yes, he saw only too well; a cheap little opportunist with the acumen to cash in when chance presented itself and the wit to place a forgotten name in the right category. She was, perhaps, more dangerous than the others.

"Astrea—" he said, his back still turned to the big music-room she had built on to the house after her husband's death, "there have been so many others, all out for what they could get. After each fiasco you said you would listen to me next time. Will you never learn?"

She fell back, as she always did when she was getting the worst of the argument, on financial matters.

"I'm in a position to pay for my mistakes," she said regally. "My own considerable earnings went long ago, we know, but Stubbs left me all that money. I can afford to indulge my whims."

He did not reply immediately. She was, of course, perfectly right when she said she was in a position to pay for her mistakes. He had been too young at the time to remember the furore caused by Astrea's decision to leave the operatic stage in order to marry Albert Stubbs, the famous sausage king. She had been married before, of course, twice, by her own rather vague reckoning, but neither marriage had interfered with her career, and it was said that her voice was beginning to go when she met Stubbs. She always alluded to him by his surname, as if he had been some kind of employee, and now she had been widowed for fifteen years with, it was said, a considerable fortune at her disposal.

"You can't expect," he said at last, "that I can enjoy seeing you being exploited."

"My dear boy," she retorted with the old imperious spirit, "the great ones of this earth are always exploited. Fame has its penalties as well as its glories."

He was too wise now to point out that her face was forgotten, but her money was an ever-present temptation. His aunt's vagaries exasperated him beyond measure, but he was very fond of her.

He turned slowly back to the warmth and brightness of the big room with its grand piano, vast gramophone, and record-filled cabinets. The walls were hung with photo-

graphs of Astrea taken in various operatic rôles, and framed
programs of concerts adorned with the famous signatures
of the artists taking part. Mementos of past glories were
everywhere, and Marc's rather hard eyes held a look of
sadness as they travelled over the familiar objects. The
room was like a shrine, he thought irritably, his eyes coming to rest on the flamboyant figure of his aunt, leaning in
a singer's pose against the piano.

She was so quick to catch the mood of another and turn it
to her advantage, that already the corners of her carelessly
painted mouth were drooping.

"There's no one left but you, Marc," she said, extend-
ing her arms in supplication with a jangle of charm-hung
bracelets. "Would you deny an old woman her harmless
extravagances?"

"They aren't all harmless," he retorted grimly. "What
about the young woman who nearly got you to alter your
will in her favor, or the poor clergyman's daughter who
made off with your diamond tiara?"

"I should have been warned by the stars," she said in a
tone of dismissal. "One was Cancer and the other Pisces,
both antagonistic to my own Sign. Your profession
naturally makes you suspicious, dear boy, but you mustn't
let your court-room triumphs thin the good red blood in
your veins. You are thirty-six, Marc. Young for such success at the Bar, I admit, but a dangerous age for settling
into the critical habits of bachelordom. You should be
thinking of marriage."

His resolute mouth twitched a little at the corners. It had
always been her practice to turn the tables on himself. She
was an adept at trailing a red herring across an unwelcome
discussion.

"My one inclination towards marriage didn't receive
much encouragement, as you very well know," he replied a
little dryly. "Let's not confuse the issue."

"Ah, Roma . . ." she said, ignoring the hint. "You know that was my dearest wish, but the poor child was afraid of poverty."

His eyebrows rose.

"I was scarcely poor, even then, except by your standards, perhaps," he retorted. "But I've no doubt an American chain-store magnate proved an irresistible temptation."

"Roma was my adopted daughter in all but the legal sense," Astrea said. "My money would have come to her had she married you. It was you who were difficult then."

"I did not care for future expectations to be the deciding factor as to whether a young woman would consent to marry me or not," he said with sudden hauteur. "I was making a comfortable enough income even seven years ago."

"But Roma was ambitious," she pleaded. "I had spoilt her with too much luxury. She was so exquisite, so gay, and now she is widowed, poor child, and you have never married. Perhaps she will return to us."

"With all her American dollars? No, Astrea, put that sort of romantic notion aside. In any case, I thought you hadn't forgiven her for running off to the States with Wilbur G. Nixon."

"No, I haven't. She hurt me very much. Still, she's older now, and—I miss her, Marc."

His eyes were gentle.

"And this series of unsuitable companions have just been filling in the gap?"

"Perhaps . . . I don't know. I get bored, with only Minnie to talk to—besides, she's getting old."

"H'm . . . and what does Minnie say to this latest folly?"

"Folly?" Her heavily pencilled eyebrows rose in displeasure for a moment, then she smiled reluctantly.

"Oh, you know Minnie—grumbles one minute and relents the next. She doesn't understand I need youth around me, now Roma's gone."

"You could entertain."

"No, no, it's not the same. People think I'm eccentric, and no one remembers. They come for what they can get. I prefer my memories and someone to share them with. The new girl at least has an appreciation of music. Her father, she tells me, was once connected with the operatic world— a composer of no distinction, I understand—but he gave his daughter a musical education of sorts. If she fits in with our life at Cleat, I might adopt her legally."

"Have you already suggested that?"

She heard the sharpness in his voice and looked up at him with a twinge of apprehension. He was her nephew and in no way officially concerned with how she chose to lead her life, but she had heard him in court many times and recognized the cold resolution which could somehow manage to frustrate her more extravagant humors, however much she chose to ignore it. She looked into the dark, angular face so like his father's, with its long nose and straight mouth, saw the sudden alertness in the bright, shrewd eyes, and mentally placed a barrister's wig on the dark hair, and grimaced.

"Naturally not," she replied, matching his own displeasure. "I have only met her once—met her and engaged her," she finished firmly.

He gave an infinitesimal shrug of resignation.

"Very well," he said. "What's her name?"

"Charity Child."

"For heaven's sake, aunt! Are you as gullible as that?"

"I don't know what you mean. An unusual name, perhaps, but rather charming, don't you think?"

"So unusual that she must have invented it on the spot.

Charity Child, indeed! Was she by any chance reared in an orphanage?"

"Not that I'm aware of. How suspicious you are, Marc. I can understand Roma's hesitance now."

But he was not going to be sidetracked by the mention of Roma's name a second time.

"But she was down to her last shilling, wasn't she?" he persisted. "You had lost her her job, so the landlady couldn't be paid, I suppose. How much did you give her?"

"Only a month's salary in advance. Really, Marc, I consider you are being very high-handed. Used you to treat Roma to this sort of cross-examination?"

"Never mind Roma. I doubt you'll hear anything further from your precious Charity what's-her-name. What day did you say she was supposed to arrive?"

"Tomorrow—Friday."

"It's Friday today," he told her grimly. "You know very well I've come for the weekend."

"Oh!" She clapped her hand to her mouth in a gesture reminiscent of a child. She was notoriously vague and absent-minded. "What's the time? I ordered the taxi for *tomorrow* — to meet the 6:15. The poor child must be sitting on the platform, wondering what has happened. You can never get a taxi from the village at this hour. Marc, would you—?"

"Certainly I'll go and fetch her—if she's there to collect," he said with sardonic pleasure. "I have a notion that I might put the fear of God into Miss Charity Child on the drive back from the station."

She made an imperious gesture.

"Now, Marc, you're not to alarm her. She is thin and undernourished, and doesn't look very strong."

"Indeed? And how else do I recognize her besides picking out the most undernourished passenger?"

"You can't miss her," Astrea said simply, gazing with sudden wistfulness at an imaginary property moon in the ceiling. "She has a face like a sad pierrot."

"Oh, really, aunt!" Marc exclaimed in disgust, and left the room with ungentle exasperation.

IT WAS a matter of eight miles to the nearest station, time enough, he thought grimly, to strip this little charlatan of pretences, should she, indeed, turn up at all, which he very much doubted. He had dealt, in due course, with most of his aunt's other protégées without much trouble, but it would be infinitely more satisfactory to nip this affair in the bud before Astrea, as always happened, found she had been had for a sucker.

He was too annoyed to appreciate the beauty of the still February night, the gentle downs and the dark folds of the distant Weald which, for years, had never failed to delight him. Cleat had been his second home for a long time, for his aunt was his only living relative and it was pleasant to commute between her house and his own London flat, spending much of his vacations there, lazing after a term's arduous work.

He was, in his way, as solitary as she, and, that unhappy affair of seven years ago set finally aside, he had lost his bitterness in work rather than the many alternative distractions that offered, and made a considerable name for himself in legal circles. Briefs had piled up, and at thirty-six he was already considering taking silk. A brilliant pleader in court, it was said of him; women thought him a cold fish and frequently told him so. Only Astrea penetrated sometimes under the hard shell, but although she frequently chided him on his bachelor state, he knew that since he had not married Roma, his aunt was secretly pleased that he continued to remain single.

Marc pulled up in the deserted station yard and almost immediately he saw the girl. For once his aunt had been right, and the absurd description fitted. The girl was sitting on a suitcase in a graceful curve of melancholy, staring up at the moon, and, by a trick of light perhaps, her face had the white traditional conception of Pierrot. She was bareheaded and even the hair clung closely to her head resembling a tight black skull-cap.

Marc shrugged a little angrily as he got out of the car and prepared to introduce himself. He had been genuinely convinced that the girl, having made an easy killing, would fail to show up; well, she was probably after bigger game.

"Is your name—Charity Child?" he asked, boggling a little over the flagrant absurdity of the invention.

She looked slowly up at him, and her eyes seemed dark and enormous in her white face. She regarded him gravely before replying and his temper rose as he realized she was considering the advisability of making any reply at all.

"Yes," she said then. "Has Mrs. Stubbs sent you to meet me?"

Her voice was soft and quite composed. It was, he thought, difficult to assess her age, but she was younger than he had expected.

"I'm her nephew, Marc Gentle," he replied with a discouraging absence of welcome in his voice. "My aunt ordered a taxi to meet your train, but she mistook the day."

For a moment her face showed vivid interest and the clown's likeness was lost.

"The barrister?" she asked. "Your aunt spoke of you, and sometimes I've followed your cases in the press."

"You're interested in the course of justice, then?" he replied a little grimly, and she looked puzzled.

"Not very, I suppose, but I enjoy reading a brilliant speech," she said.

"Do you, indeed? Well, Miss Charity Child, we'd better be moving. Is this all your luggage?"

"Yes. You say my name as if it was a kind of joke, Mr. Gentle."

"I've an idea you made it up, Miss Child," he said with polite contempt, and as she slowly uncoiled her long legs and stood up, he picked up her suitcase and slung it carelessly into the back of the car. He did not trouble to open the passenger's door for her; indeed, it gave him satisfaction to match her own unexpected politeness with most unaccustomed discourtesy.

She withdrew into her corner, aware of, though puzzled by, his antagonism. Her long legs disposed themselves with grace, he noticed, and her profile, against the window, was again the face of Pierrot, a black-and-white etching, remote and withdrawn.

He drove slowly, aware that now was the moment for the things he wanted to say.

"My aunt has engaged you as her companion, I understand," he began with misleading pleasantness.

"Yes," she said. "It was all rather sudden, but—it seemed wonderful to me to work for someone like that."

"Astrea's name meant something to you, then? She was at the peak of her fame long before you were born."

"Yes, I suppose so. But my father had records. He used to say she might have been another Flagstadt had her voice not gone so early. My father knew about such things. He was a musician himself."

His eyebrows rose slightly.

"Indeed? You had, of course, free access to the record library where you worked," he observed suavely.

"Oh, yes," she said, sounding surprised, "but the firm didn't stock much classical stuff. I doubt if there was one of Astrea's old records among the lot."

He changed gear a little roughly.

"And yet you knew her?" he said.

Charity smiled, looking out into the frost-encrusted fields and hedges. The quiet countryside was so peaceful after the bustle of London, the blaring records in the music shop, the cramped drabness of the digs which had been her only home. It was difficult to concentrate on what this unexpected and rather hostile stranger was saying. She had a moment's impression of the eccentric old woman who had swept into the shop, with her dyed hair and jangling charms, turning the place out for some record they did not possess and being subjected to the greasy little manager's insolence. Charity herself had become embroiled because the name of Astrea had meant something from the past: the loss of her job, the subsequent extraordinary interview in a neighboring teashop, still seemed like a bizarre dream.

"Of course not," she said. "But I remembered her name from things my father had told me, and—well, there's still something of the prima donna about her, isn't there?"

Marc felt an irrational anger rising in him. Was this chit trying to put him in his place?

"I think you should know, Miss Child, that my aunt is given to these sudden whims," he said. "There is no promise of permanence, or other material benefits—no matter how inviting the proposition may have sounded."

"Naturally that is understood," she answered, sounding surprised. "Is Mrs. Stubbs regretting her impulsiveness?"

"Not at the moment, but she will. In case you should imagine that you are first in the field, I had better point out that there have been others—all ready to cash in on my aunt's gullibility."

There was no doubt, now, of his hostility. Charity did not yet quite grasp the full extent of his cynical warnings, but she felt the blood begin to mount under her skin.

"I don't think I quite understand you," she said, still striving after politeness.

They had reached the crest of a hill and he suddenly pulled into the side of the road and stopped his engine. Beneath them the country dropped into a gentle valley with the lights of the cottages twinkling in the darkness. Beyond, where the road wound steeply up again, lay Cleat House in its isolation, with Astrea, at that very moment, waiting to clasp her newest protégée to her generous bosom.

"We had better understand each other once and for all," Marc said, turning to face the girl. "Unlike my aunt, I have a considerable experience of the cupidity of human nature, and I'm warning you now that although you may have pulled the wool over her eyes, you won't pull it over mine. Is that understood?"

She shrank back into her corner of the car and her eyes seemed to stretch more widely still in her white face.

"You—you think I'm exploiting your aunt's kindness?" she stammered.

"Something like that."

"But *why*? It was unconventional, perhaps, accepting a job from a perfect stranger, but—I hadn't much choice in the circumstances."

"On your beam ends—that's what you told her, didn't you?"

"Not quite. I would have found another job eventually."

"But this was so much easier? You had, after all, only to flatter her by pretending to remember her name."

"Don't you believe I did?"

"No, I'm afraid I don't. Astrea was at the height of her fame nearly forty years ago."

There was a little silence, then she asked in a small, quiet voice:

"Are you musical, Mr. Gentle?"

"Not particularly," he replied, viewing her averted profile with sardonic amusement.

"Then you wouldn't realize, perhaps, that the great names still live. Caruso, Melba, Clara Butt—all before my time—and yours too, if it comes to that. Why should it seem odd that Astrea's name is known to me?" She spoke with a composure that annoyed him. He had not been prepared for argument, or for his own uneasy sense of uncertainty.

"Her fame was short-lived," he answered tersely. "It's only reasonable to suppose that, except for a lucky break, you would never have heard of her."

"A lucky break?"

He had lighted a cigarette, and now tossed it, half-smoked, through the window.

"Yes," he said, and knew an irrational desire to shake her. "My aunt invariably announces herself to strangers. It's only reasonable conjecture that someone in a firm of music publishers, however ill-informed, would have heard of her name. It would appear that yours were the quick wits to make use of the knowledge."

At last she turned to look at him, and in the bright moonlight he saw her eyes were not brown, or even black, as he had first supposed, but a very dark grey, with the strange untroubled innocence of a child's, and as he watched, they slowly filled with tears.

"What you're trying to say is you believe I seized the opportunity and then invented a hard-luck story," she said quietly.

"Something like that."

The tears trembled on her lashes, but did not fall, and he was conscious of disappointment. He would have liked to reduce her to tears as he had reduced so many women in the witness box.

She turned away again.

"Do you live with your aunt, Mr. Gentle?" she enquired politely.

"Not permanently. Why?"

"Only that if you did I think it would be better if I took another job," she said, and he laughed without amusement.

"It may yet come to that," he retorted. "I come down most weekends, so I'll be holding a watching brief. Well, I think we understand each other now, Miss Charity Child. I've warned you; the rest is up to you."

For some strange reason it was only then that he really pierced her composure. Her slender body seemed to shrink into the semblance of a child's, and when she spoke it was with a cornered child's defiance.

"I think," she said, "you are the most disagreeable man I've ever met! You seem to find *my* name funny, but you hardly live up to yours, do you? A less gentle person I've never known in my life!"

"*Well*—" he said softly, and his mouth softened in an involuntary smile "—plain speaking all round! I wondered when I was going to get under your skin. But be warned, my dear—I'm up to most of the tricks of little girls like you."

"I'm not likely to forget," she retorted, then added, as he started up his engine: "And I'll warn *you*, Mr. Gentle— you can be caught by your own cleverness—never mind the tricks of other people."

He smiled again, a trifle grimly this time, and putting the car into gear, drove up the steep hill to Cleat House.

To Charity, the joy of the day had gone, for it had held joy, this adventure into the unknown. Astrea's impetuous offer had not seemed strange to her, used as she had been to her father's often disastrous impulses before he died. Since then life had seemed drab and unrewarding without the color of that beloved personality; the struggle for existence had not been easy, and the offer of a job that would bring some of that color back had sounded heaven-sent.

She had liked the odd old prima donna whom nobody remembered, and had sensed some of the loneliness of spirit of the forgotten ones of the earth. It was a shock for which she had been quite unprepared, to be met by this suspicious and unpleasant stranger, and learn what the world might think of her innocent motives.

She sat beside him, fighting back the tears, and after that, everything became confused. They stopped at a house with vaguely Gothic proportions, and immediately the door was thrown open and there was Astrea, vast and welcoming, folding her at once in an enveloping embrace as if she was the prodigal returned.

"My dear, dear child . . ." she cried extravagantly, "what joy that you are here! Come in, come in . . . my home is yours, and you shall be a daughter to me, if you will."

Even to Charity, the greeting smacked of histrionics, but the warmth could not be denied, and the tears she had been keeping back fell, despite her.

"What!" cried Astrea, her own eyes filling at once. "Tears of gratitude, already? What sensitivity—what responsiveness! But Aquarians are highly sensitive. Come, my child, my home awaits you."

Charity was aware of Marc watching them, his dark face cynical in the sudden flood of light. She could have bitten her tongue out for betraying emotion in front of him, an emotion which he, all too plainly, took to be a histrionic compliment to that of his aunt. She drew away from Astrea's submerging embrace and sniffed inelegantly, like a chidden child.

"Well," he observed, closing the front door on the frosty night, "now you have both cried on each other's shoulder, I trust there is mutual satisfaction. Where shall I put the luggage, Astrea?"

"Roma's old room, of course. I always put them there."

Marc's glance at Charity was grimly amused as he picked up her suitcase.

"You see, Miss Charity Child, you are only one of many," he said as he began to mount the stairs.

"First," said Astrea, ignoring him, "you must meet Minnie, then I will show you your room. It is very important that you should get on with Minnie, for she rules our lives here. She used to be my dresser long ago—now she runs the house for me."

She rang a bell and presently a small wizened old woman emerged somewhere from the back regions of the house and stood there, waiting, without saying a word. She was probably younger than her mistress, Charity thought, but her skin was wrinkled and her hair an uncompromising grey. Minnie would never have fought the advancing years with fashionable hair-styles and clothes. She wore what she would have described, herself, as decent black and a small, frilled apron.

"This is Miss Child, of whom I spoke to you," Astrea said with a vague wave of one heavily ringed hand. "You will make her welcome, I hope, Minnie. The stars are most propitious for her advent among us."

The little old woman looked at Charity, and her bright, expressionless glance was as unresponsive as Marc's had been.

"You said tomorrow," she replied, without proffering any greeting or acknowledgment. "It'll be short common in the dining room tonight, with Mr. Marc in the house."

"Don't be so absurd!" Astrea exclaimed impatiently. "Since when has an extra guest made any difference at Cleat?"

"Since you took to cutting down on the groceries and suchlike," Minnie replied promptly and, without waiting for further instructions, turned her back and made off for the kitchen.

"Such nonsense!" Astrea boomed in her throaty voice, shepherding Charity upstairs. "Just because, like all old servants, she's extravagant! Are you a big eater, my dear?"

"No, I don't think so," Charity answered, beginning to feel exhausted.

"Good, good. I, myself, am on a diet. Virgo subjects benefit from seed-bearing plants, nuts, and vegetables which grow above ground. We share that with the Gemini types. I must look up the foodstuffs that are ruled by Aquarius so that you can benefit, too."

Following her hostess or employer—it was not very clear which at present—through the house, Charity hoped the diet prescribed by the stars for her would not also prove to be one of nuts. She enjoyed her food when, as had been rare, she was able to indulge in mild extravagance.

The house seemed filled with ill-assorted furniture, Oriental cabinets of hideous design rubbing shoulders with Georgian and Queen Anne, worthless knick-knacks everywhere, the whole producing a somewhat cosmopolitan air which accorded badly with the solid proportions of the rooms.

"You are admiring my treasures?" Astrea said. "So many souvenirs of my European tours—so many gifts from admirers—a lifetime's history in all of them."

Charity privately wondered how anything got dusted, then decided that Astrea could not be fussy as a cloud of dust rose from hangings as they brushed by.

"And here is your own little nest," Astrea continued, flinging open a door, and Charity exlaimed involuntarily:

"What a charming room!"

It was indeed more than that, she thought, gazing about her with astonished eyes. Unlike the rest of the house, which seemed to be a hotch-potch of taste and style, this room was gracious in design. Each piece of furniture was perfect of its period, bedspread and curtains were of finest brocade and the dressing table laden with crystal bottles and trinket boxes. It was a room which might have been furnished with loving care for a favorite daughter, and Charity, remembering, wondered who Roma was.

But Astrea was already exclaiming in annoyance at the absence of a fire.

"Really, Minnie is becoming impossible!" she said. "No fire to welcome you on a night like this, and no flowers, either!"

"She thought I was coming tomorrow," Charity reminded her shyly. "Besides, Mrs. Stubbs, I shouldn't think paid companions expect those sort of attentions."

"Astrea, my dear child . . . you must call me Astrea . . ." the older woman replied absently. "And you must not think of yourself in those terms. What is money, when all is said and done?"

Charity was inclined to retort that it could represent considerable importance to the wage-earners of this world, but she said instead,

"You are being so very kind. This lovely room—did it belong to someone dear to you?"

"My spiritual daughter," Astrea answered dreamily. "Yes, she was very dear to me . . ."

"And did she die?" Charity asked softly, her heart going out to someone who was, like herself, bereaved.

"Oh, dear me, no," Astrea replied briskly. "She married and went to America—not at all the same thing, is it? You shall take her place, my child. Yes, you are more *simpatica* than Roma—you shall take her place."

Charity had an uneasy recollection that there had been others before her, all occupying Roma's room, all, perhaps, intended for the nebulous rôle of spiritual daughter, and for a fleeting moment she could sympathize with the blunt misgivings of the disagreeable nephew.

She spoke a little stiffly because she was embarrassed.

"I hope I shall give satisfaction," she said. "You didn't say what my duties would be."

"Didn't I?" answered Astrea vaguely. "Oh, arranging flowers, telephoning, shopping, perhaps—and you will play for me, of course. We will renew the past with music—I might even sing again. . . . Come, dear child, unpack your things and come downstairs to the music-room—through the hall and straight down the passage to your right. I use it instead of a drawing room, for it expresses my personality. Now, hurry, child. Dinner is at eight o'clock, and Marc likes his glass of sherry first. Did you like him?"

"There was scarcely time to form an opinion," said Charity guardedly, whose opinion had, indeed, been very forcibly formed in that brief interview.

"That will, of course, be remedied very soon, but don't expect attentions. He wanted to marry Roma at one time, but now women don't attract him. So brilliant, you know, and much run after, so I believe, only . . ." Astrea had drifted towards the door as she talked and it closed behind her, cutting off her final sentence.

Charity unpacked her few possessions and laid them carefully away in Roma's lovely drawers and cupboards, remembering her father's delight in the beautiful things he could never afford. They had lived in cheap lodgings and furnished houses all her life, but he had taught her a secondhand appreciation of beauty and elegance. She was suddenly passionately grateful to Astrea for opening the door, however briefly, on a world which had always been just out of reach.

She found the music-room without much trouble and Marc rose politely from his chair to offer her a glass of sherry. There was, she felt uncomfortably, still hostility beneath the courtesy, and mockery, too. In the bright lights of the music-room she could see him in perspective for the first time, and disliked still further what she saw.

He possessed a vague kind of elegance that gave him a
fastidious air; the dark, angular face was distinguished in a
cold, legal sense, she supposed, but the shrewd eyes would
strip you unmercifully, and she knew, by his reputation,
how well he could tear a witness's evidence to shreds. An
implacable enemy and an uncomfortable friend, she
thought, and wished her first evening at Cleat could have
been rid of his presence.

Dinner, when it was served, was, despite Minnie's
threats, ample and well-planned. Astrea ate her nuts with
no very great enjoyment, but Marc and Charity did full
justice to the fare provided for them. Minnie was clearly an
excellent cook.

"Do you permit your companions wine?" Marc asked,
having filled his aunt's and his own glasses, and, although
he phrased the question with wry humor, Charity knew he
was reminding her that she had no family status in the
house.

"Naturally," Astrea replied. "Charity is a little different from the others, as you can see, dear boy. That little
girl from Brighton could never appreciate a good vintage and the one who followed her drank too much. Fill
the child's glass."

"I don't drink, thank you," said Charity clearly, and he
paused beside her chair with raised eyebrows.

"No?" he said sceptically.

"No."

He shrugged and sat down again, and Astrea leaned
across the table in the candlelight.

"Marc does not approve of what he pleases to call my
whims," she said. "You mustn't let him embarrass you,
my dear."

"Mr. Gentle, I think, fears that your kindness and good
nature may become exploited," Charity answered politely,
and Marc's mouth tightened. So she was ready to do battle

with him in the open, was she, the cool little minx? Very well, let her know where she stood.

"Unfortunately, human nature is easily gulled—haven't you found that, Miss Child?" he said suavely, but was unprepared for the grave regard she turned upon him.

"No," she said gently, "I've always found people take you very much as they find you, but I haven't, of course, your insight into human nature."

"*Touché!*" Astrea exclaimed delightedly, and gave a deep burst of throaty laughter.

Marc's answering smile was a trifle grim, but he inclined his head graciously towards Charity, and sat watching her in silence. In the faintly distorting light of the candles the Pierrot illusion was extraordinary; the plaintive brows and the thick black lashes looked artificial in her white face. She was even wearing a dress with some absurd dark toby frill at the neck, and he wondered, with sudden irritation, if she knew of the teasing resemblance and dressed to emphasize it. Her composure was unusual and a little disturbing, then she looked up, suddenly aware of his regard, and he saw, for a fleeting moment, that she was not composed at all, only young and puzzled, and a little alarmed. He saw, too, the instant hostility spring into her eyes before she lowered her lashes again.

"How old are you?" he asked, and his voice had momentarily lost its antagonistic mockery.

"Twenty."

"Your birthday must fall between the twentieth of January and the eighteenth of February. When was it?" Astrea asked with sudden intensity.

"Well, actually, it's the day after tomorrow—Sunday," Charity answered reluctantly.

Astrea clapped her hands together, and her old eyes held a child's delight.

"Then you are still nineteen—a child, like Ganymede,

the shepherd-boy who is indentified with your Sign—Aquarius, the Water Bearer!" she exclaimed. "How fitting that you should spend your birthday here! Marc, we must celebrate . . . but so little time, so little time . . . tomorrow we will go to Brighton and plunder the shops, and Minnie shall prepare a special feast—and a cake. So much to think of . . . I must go at once and speak to Minnie. . . ."

"Oh, please—" Charity began, distressed at so much attention being focussed upon her, but Astrea had already gone, leaving the two of them to an uncomfortable silence and their unfinished sweet course.

"Well!" Marc said softly. "You've certainly timed your entrance very well, Miss Charity Child."

For the first time she was driven to plain rudeness with him.

"I think you're altogether hateful!" she said. "Do you imagine I wanted to mention my birthday—to have a fuss? Do you suspect everyone your aunt employs of trying to feather their own nests? You may be a very clever lawyer, Mr. Gentle, but you should have learnt by now, I should have thought, to discriminate."

She banged her spoon and fork on to her plate, leaving her sweet unfinished, and sat glowering at him in the candlelight.

His eyes rested on her for a moment, seeing the reticence in her face, and being vaguely troubled by it. If he had misjudged her, then she might suffer quite considerably from Astrea's whims and fancies.

"Perhaps you should know—" he began a little awkwardly, but his aunt came back into the room with the gusty ebullience which characterized all her entrances.

"Minnie is making a sour mouth about it, of course," she announced, "but she'll come round, as she always does. Now, let us go to the music-room for coffee, and discuss our plans. How fortunate Marc will be here for your birthday, my dear child—so much more amusing for you than a sabbath's sojourn with an old woman. Are you ready, Marc? We will persuade Charity to play for us.''

Marc and Charity pushed back their chairs and stood for a moment in the failing light of the guttering candles. They were part of the background, Charity thought, watching Marc and his aunt; they could not know that it was her first experience of candlelight spilling on old silver and polished mahogany, of damask napkins and fine glass, of the leisurely formality of a meal prepared by other hands. She was a stranger amongst them, an alien to their way of life, and, in Marc Gentle's eyes, a character that was already suspect.

"Would you mind, Mrs. Stubbs, if I went to bed?" she asked, and saw Astrea's mouth drop in disappointment.

"Astrea, dear," she replied automatically. "And not play for us, Charity? I was looking forward to an evening reviving my memories.''

Charity hesitated. If she was being employed as a companion, her duty clearly lay in obliging her employer, but Marc interposed smoothly:

"The girl is probably tired. There will be time and enough to spare for music when I have gone.''

It was pleasantly spoken but, glanced at his rather forbidding face, Charity thought that he, as much as she, wanted to end this ill-assorted threesome.

"Of course," Astrea said, but she looked put out. "I trust you will sleep well. I, of course, always sleep with my head to the magnetic north—so vital to well-being. We can move your bed, if you wish.''

"Please don't trouble," said Charity, who had never heard of the advantages of the magnetic north. "Goodnight, Mr. Gentle.''

"Goodnight, Miss Child," Marc returned gravely, and

watched her leave the room and, through the wrought-iron banisters, saw her long, slim legs climbing the stairs.

"Well," he said, turning to his aunt, "you will have to make do with me for the rest of the evening, I'm afraid."

"So ridiculous!" Astrea said crossly. "Do you suppose she's not strong, Marc?"

"You told me yourself she looked undernourished," he reminded her unkindly.

"Did I? Even so, the very first evening she should have been willing to fulfil the functions of a companion, don't you think?"

"You've been treating her like a guest, not a companion, Astrea," he said gently, and, as he followed her to the music-room, wondered, with wry humor, which of them most needed protecting from the other.

CHAPTER TWO

CHARITY SLEPT well in the most comfortable bed she had ever known, but her waking thoughts were not of Astrea, the miraculous source of so much felicity, but of the unpleasant nephew who so plainly resented her and whose weekend visits, she knew without doubt, were going to prove a very large thorn in her well-being. But the morning brought fresh contentment. The downs beyond her window sparkled with sunshine and frost, and Minnie brought up early tea, a luxury Charity had never known before.

"You mustn't do this for me," she said shyly. "I'm used to getting up early in the morning and doing a job."

Minnie regarded her with that expressionless stare which Charity felt, took in so much more than was apparent.

"Madam's orders," she replied. "Never learn, will that one. Paid companions waited on as if they was gentry."

"I don't expect to be waited on," said Charity, withdrawing a little against her pillows. "I'm sure you've enough to do without that, Minnie."

"Soft-soap me, would you?" the old woman retorted uncompromisingly. "What I does for you is only for Madam's sake, see? Not but what you won't lap it up, to the manner born, same as the others."

She went away then, and Charity sighed. It was not pleasant to be resented, and so far only Astrea, it would seem, had shown welcome for her.

When she was dressed she went downstairs to seek breakfast and found Marc eating alone in the rather gloomy dining room. She dutifully bade him good morning, and when he did not reply, turned towards a side-table to help herself from the various chafing dishes.

"Not one of the orange juice brigade, I'm glad to see," he observed without looking up from his paper. "You slept well?"

"Yes, thank you. Does Mrs. Stubbs not come down for breakfast?"

"No—and she'll be very annoyed if you continue to address her as Mrs. Stubbs. You'd better try to remember."

"I'm sorry," Charity said, and at the same moment Astrea erupted into the room, presenting a strange appearance in an ancient négligé over which she wore a puce cardigan and sundry scarves. Her dyed hair was still in curlers, and her face unadorned except for hastily applied mascara.

"Marc, you will take us to Brighton, I trust?" she said, seizing an apple from a dish in passing. "I shall hurry my toilette today for that reason. We will lunch at the Metropole and then do the shops and visit the fortune-teller on the pier."

"There will hardly be a fortune-teller at this time of the year, will there?" Marc seemed quite unsurprised.

"No—no, perhaps not. Charity, dear child, have you made a list of your presents?"

"My presents?" Charity sounded bewildered, and Astrea waved her hands airily over the breakfast table. Although she was clearly just out of bed, she still wore her rings and her bracelets with their tinkling charms.

"But of course! It's your birthday tomorrow and you must make a long list—not that the local shops will have much choice. Perhaps we should wait and go to London on Monday."

"I'm sure that would be best," her nephew murmured, but at any hint of opposition, Astrea became immediately resolute.

"No, no!" she cried. "It wouldn't be the same at all—a birthday cannot pass without gifts. Now, dear child, what would you like? A fur coat, a fitted dressing-case, a bicycle, perhaps? Or can you drive a car?"

"But, Mrs. Stubbs—Astrea, I mean—presents like that are out of the question—besides, I don't want anything, truly I don't."

Charity caught Marc's expression of cynical enjoyment and, later, thought she understood it, for when in the afternoon they made a hurried round of the Brighton shops, Astrea quickly tired of the proceedings, hurriedly bought a pair of cheap nylons and a gaudy sponge-bag and left her nephew to pay the bill.

Charity caught his eye as they left the shop and burst out laughing. His answering grin was wholly spontaneous, and for the first time she felt they were in accord, but in the evening, waiting for Astrea to join them in the music-room before dinner, he observed with his old mockery:

"I hope you weren't disappointed that no fur coats materialized. My aunt likes to make grand gestures. I'm afraid they are apt to be misunderstood by the people who have had false hopes raised in their bosoms."

"I would have felt most uncomfortable if your aunt had spent a lot of money on me," said Charity stiffly, and he raised one eyebrow.

"Would you, Miss Child?" he replied with a slight drawl. "Your predecessors didn't all show your restraint—in fact I may say some of them managed to line their nests quite nicely, despite poor Astrea's proverbial parsimony."

She decided to ignore this obvious dig and exclaimed with genuine surprise:

"Parsimony? But your aunt has a most generous nature."

"Oh, I grant you that, when it suits her, but she has the foibles of the wealthy—cuts down on food one minute and foots a gigantic bill at the Ritz the next. Not to be relied upon, you see.''

''If you're trying to warn me off—'' she began indignantly, but, perhaps rather fortunately, they were interrupted by Astrea herself, her evening make-up hurriedly applied with startling results, and her out-of-date gown more suitable to a ballroom than a quiet dinner at home.

''I wore this for one of my concert recitals nearly thirty years ago,'' she said, catching Charity's look of faint surprise. ''I wear out all my old professional clothes in the evenings—so foolish to buy new, don't you think? Now, this evening we will have some music, yes?''

It was, of course, impossible to refuse, and although Charity was very loth to display her small talent in front of Marc, she sat down obediently at the piano after dinner. It was a beautiful instrument and soon she was able to forget the unresponsive figure by the fire. She played well by ear and was able to meet most of Astrea's demands for operatic *arias* and the better known German *lieder*. At intervals she found herself embraced while Astrea's fluid emotions found release in easy tears. It was all rather bewildering and a little embarrassing, and she became suddenly very conscious of Marc's silent attention, of his long, supercilious nose, and the little smile of sardonic amusement which hovered about his mouth.

Astrea suddenly wearied and flung herself into a chair on the other side of the fireplace and Marc said unexpectedly:

''You play very well. Are you good enough to take it up professionally?''

''Oh, no,'' Charity answered with a smile. ''I just have a certain facility, that's all. There's no room for the gifted amateur these days.''

''How sensible of you to know your limitations, my dear,'' said Astrea approvingly. ''I never knew mine—not that I had any, of course.''

Marc smiled.

"But naturally—you were Astrea," he said with a graciousness that sounded sincere. "Will you give us something of your own to finish up with, Charity Child?"

She was grateful for the implied compliment, and knowing, on his own admission, that he was not really musically inclined, began to play one of the familiar French nursery songs of her childhood.

> *Au clair de la lune*
> *Mon ami Pierrot . . .*

When she had finished playing she saw Marc watching her with narrowed eyes and was instantly aware of a change in his mood.

"Why did you pick on that?" he asked sharply.

"But for obvious reasons!" cried Astrea. " 'Mon ami Pierrot . . . ' charming, charming . . . did I not tell you at once of the resemblance, Marc?"

"What resemblance?" Charity asked, bewildered by both of them.

"To Pierrot," Astrea replied, delighted with her own word picture. "I said to Marc, when he was to meet you at the station, that he would know you becuase you had a face like a sad pierrot. He thought, no doubt, I was being extravagant, but it's true, isn't it, dear boy?"

Marc made no reply, but simply smiled, not very pleasantly, and Charity felt herself flushing. He thought she had chosen the song deliberately, playing up to Astrea's romantic notions, she told herself angrily, and wished she had been inspired by any other than that plaintive little air. She sat irresolutely on the piano stool, twisting her fingers together, then as Marc rather deliberately started a conversation that would exclude her, she closed the piano and went to sit in an unobtrusive corner of the room.

Astrea made a great to-do of Charity's birthday, in-

sisting on champagne and an orgy of music, and producing
small gifts from her trinket box, an old-fashioned locket, a
coral bracelet with a broken clasp, and a very charming
string of tiny pearls which she hastily snatched back and
replaced with a brooch set with a rather indifferent
amethyst.

"But that, of course, is the right stone for Aquarius,
dear child!" she cried. "You must always wear it to bring
you good fortune. My own stone is the sardonyx—so
uninteresting. I was born under Virgo, you know—Astrea,
the star-maiden, daughter of Jupiter. I took it as my professional name, naturally. My ruling planet is Mercury,
which accounts for so much, don't you think?"

Charity knew little about astrology and she found
Astrea's changes of mood bewildering. So far, nothing had
been said as to the duties which might be expected of a
companion, and, when Charity timidly asked, her queries
were waved aside as if they were merely frivolous.

"Later . . . later . . ." Astrea answered vaguely. "You
shall be a daughter to me, my child—a spiritual daughter
as Roma once was. Ganymede, cup-bearer to the gods—is
that not a charming conceit?"

Charity thought her employer's preoccupation with the
stars and their attendant mythology might become a bit exhausting, but she earnestly did her best to follow these sudden allusions, and only felt foolish when she found Marc's
sceptical eyes upon her. She was grateful for the fact that
he had not embarrassed her by feeling obliged to produce a
birthday gift of his own, but it was an uneasy day and she
felt thankful that tomorrow was Monday and he would be
gone.

Minnie's cake was a masterpiece of icing and sugar
decorations and twenty pink candles. She carried it in
herself and watched phlegmatically while Astrea went
through the traditional birthday ritual like an excited child,

exclaiming and clapping her hands, supervising the cutting of the cake, and helping Charity blow out the candles, insistent to the point of mild hysteria that not one candle should be left burning to court disaster.

Charity felt thoroughly uncomfortable, aware of Marc's dark presence in the background, quizzing in silence the childish antics of two adult persons; then Minnie spoke, her old face creased in a loving indulgence that was both startling and revealing.

"Bless your heart, ducks, you're like a child! It might be your own birthday and you twenty years old today and all the world at your feet," she said.

Astrea's sagging features held a sudden radiance. Her hair was dishevelled and her make-up carelessly applied, but, for a moment, Charity saw her as she must have been in her heyday.

"Ah!" she said. "Such fêtes . . . such adulation . . . and so soon to end."

"People who remember you will not have forgotten," Charity said softly, and her eyes were bright with sudden tears. It was, to her, both pathetic and a little frightening, this living again in the reflected youth of others.

Astrea swooped upon her, clasping her in an emotional embrace.

"You are sent to comfort me, my little Ganymede," she said. "You will be my own lost youth."

"I seem to remember you said the same sort of thing to Roma," Marc observed with gentle irony, and Charity sent him a look of intense dislike.

"It's unkind to remind people of ill-considered statements," she said severely, and Astrea laughed, the fleeting look of wonder vanishing.

"My statements are never ill-considered," she said grandly. "Minnie, remove the tea-things if nobody wants any more. I shall go to my room until dinner time."

She swept from the room in Minnie's wake, and Charity stood fingering the broken twists of icing sugar which littered the table and wondered what to do next.

"You don't approve of me, do you?" Marc said suddenly.

She kept her eyes on the sugar pieces, piling them together in a neat little heap.

"I think you go out of your way to make people feel uncomfortable," she answered.

"You think I should have played up to my aunt's histrionics—as you did?"

She wheeled suddenly to face him, and her eyes were clear and grave and troubled.

"That wasn't a moment of histrionics," she said. "They were sharing something out of the past, she and Minnie; and Minnie saw her as she must once have been."

He observed her curiously, noticing, for perhaps the first time, the sensitivity of her young mouth, the clear directness of her eyes.

"Don't let her submerge, you, Charity Child," he said softly, "Astrea is as inconsequent as the wind and—you're a new toy."

"I thought," she said, "that you were more concerned that *she* shouldn't be exploited."

He stood regarding her reflectively, his hands thrust into his trouser pockets, and the light cast misleading shadows on the angles of his dark face.

"Very true," he replied. "But you puzzle me a little. I haven't made up my mind about you."

She flushed, flinging up her head, and he noticed that her long throat looked young and somehow defenceless.

"But I, Mr. Gentle," she retorted with a spurt of temper, "made up mine about you very quickly. I think you are detestable!"

His slow smile mocked her.

"I shouldn't let it worry you," he said.

"Worry me!"

"No, of course it wouldn't. Well, it will be interesting to see how you make out—the last, I hope, of my aunt's many mistakes. But watch your step, Charity Child, watch your step," he said, and turned, without further ado, and walked out of the room.

THE WEEK that followed brought comfort to Charity and a strange new sense of belonging. Not since her father had died had she known the interest and affection of another human being.

Astrea's path crossing hers had seemed like a portent. It had never occurred to her to doubt either the old prima donna's identity or her good faith. She had journeyed to Cleat filled with trust in the future and only that very disagreeable Marc Gentle had shaken her belief in her good fortune. It was not pleasant to be reminded of his suspicions of her intentions, or his careless hints that his aunt's impulses could prove fickle, but once rid of his presence, she thrust these thoughts behind her. He did not come down to Cleat every weekend by any means, Astrea informed her, adding, vaguely, that he had changed a good deal since Roma had married.

As the days went by Charity picked up the threads of the quiet life at Cleat with surprising ease. Astrea's whirlwind changes of mood could be bewildering and sometimes a little alarming, but her evident pleasure in the girl's company offered a balm to which she found quick response. Charity was, perhaps, too young to heed Marc's light-hearted warning that she, herself, constituted a new toy; she knew only delight in performing services, running errands, and listening to endless and highly-colored tales of the past. Even Minnie unbent sufficiently to underline accounts of her mistress's successes, although she would not permit familiarities, and was quick to put Charity in her place should she appear too contented with her lot.

"Don't you be too sure of yourself, young miss," she

said. "Easy come, easy go, that's how it's been these past few years, and not all of 'em out for what they could get, I'm bound to admit. M'lady takes fancies and tires of 'em. Seems she can't settle down since Miss Roma went."

"But marriage shouldn't alter affections," Charity said, and Minnie pulled down her mouth, sniffing scornfully.

"Ah, but 'twas Mr. Marc she was meant to wed," she replied. "Not but what that wouldn't have worked, to my way of thinking, but Madam had her heart set on it."

"Well, I can understand her disappointment," Charity said, and the old woman sniffed again.

"One's as like as the other, each wanting her own way," she said obscurely. "though Miss Roma never had the heart m'lady's got. Money, money, money! Well, she's got it now, and small good will all those Yankee dollars do her, I shouldn't wonder."

Charity pondered sometimes on the character of the unknown girl whose room she occupied and whose presence could still be felt in the house. Minnie had probably been jealous, she thought, and wondered idly how seriously the fastidious Mr. Gentle's feeling had been engaged.

She quickly became used to Astrea's idiosyncrasies; her meanness with the household bills when visitors were not expected, her alternating fads, her solemn preoccupation with signs and portents. Each morning Charity had to read aloud the stars' predictions in the many newspapers Astrea took for the purpose, and inevitably she would exclaim: "Arrant rubbish! Astrology is a science, and not intended for the masses who want to know their luck." But she took her daily press seriously enough to become upset and indecisive when, as often happened, one newspaper's forecast completely contradicted another's.

The house itself was unattractive, with its pretentious turrets and gables and the mock-Gothic design which had presumably gladdened the heart of the late Mr. Albert Stubbs, but the surrounding country was beautiful. A town-dweller all her life, Charity loved the freedom of the downs, with the wide vistas, the grazing sheep, and the dewponds. She took long walks when Astrea did not require her, enjoying the spring of turf beneath her feet and the smell of the sea on the wind.

In the evenings there was music. Astrea owned a fine collection of operatic recordings, many of which she had recorded herself. It must be strange and a little heartbreaking, Charity thought, to hear one's own voice after nearly forty years, soaring effortlessly in its prime, and know that same voice to be lost forever. Often Astrea wept, whether with regret or simple emotion it was hard to know; then she would launch into one of her many anecdotes; quarrels with other artists, contempt for more successful rivals, scandals, and the fabulous gala nights when the audience went wild and the horses were taken from the prima donna's carriage and she was pulled to her lodgings by her fervent admirers.

"But horses and carriages were surely longer ago than that," Charity protested once, and received a disapproving frown.

"I may have become confused," said Astrea shortly. "But no—in Russia there were *drotskies*, and in Vienna sleighs, or perhaps it was the other way round. It makes no matter. That was an age of gracious living, my child."

Charity did some quick mental arithmetic which brought her to the roaring 'twenties and the gracious living of bottle parties and the Charleston, Eton crops, flat chests, and the screaming Bright Young Things. She smiled with affectionate tolerance, but did not interrupt again. Indeed, however much Astrea romanced or exaggerated, Charity was an enthralled listener. She would sit at Astrea's feet in the firelight, and, for her, the evenings became an Arabian

Nights entertainment. Never in her life had she known anyone with such a vivid personality or felt herself to be part of an era only to be read of in books and journals.

In those early days they were a delightful counterpart to one another, for Astrea had never known such an avid listener, or one so ready to worship at a forgotten shrine. The others had flattered her at first but had soon wearied of events which had happened before they were born, but this child sat with her great eyes filled with wonder, ready to laugh or weep at her bidding.

"You are, indeed, my spiritual daughter," she exclaimed on one occasion. "Our stars have met, dear Ganymede, and you, I think, must be a small projection of myself, I shall leave you my money—yes, I shall leave you poor Stubb's fortune. I will ring my lawyers tomorrow."

Charity, though startled, did not take this pronouncement very seriously. Astrea, she thought shrewdly, was the kind of woman who enjoyed making grand gestures and was probably always changing her will.

"That's most kind of you," she replied politely, "but you should talk it over with your nephew when he comes at the weekend. He wouldn't, I'm sure, hear of such a thing—a stranger whom you hardly know."

"Marc has no jurisdiction over my affairs," retorted Astrea, stung, as always, by any hint of opposition. "Besides, he's not coming this weekend."

"Not?" Charity's spirits rose at once. She had not been looking forward to Mr. Marc Gentle's next visit.

"Some case pending," Astrea said vaguely. "He'll be working in chambers. Do you not care for the idea of being my heiress, dear child?"

Charity scarcely knew what to answer. She did not for a moment think that Astrea intended to ring her lawyers, but the suggestion could not be ignored altogether.

"You must have other heirs, more close to you," she said gently. "Your nephew, for instance?"

"Marc has no need for my money, he makes plenty of his own," Astrea answered impatiently. "He will, of course, as my only living relative, come in for a nice little legacy, but that will by no means account for it all. Stubbs was a rich man—all those sausages, you know—so unromantic, but necessary, I suppose. I cannot bear to eat sausages for that reason, though Minnie likes them. Roma would have had my money had she married Marc."

Charity frowned.

"You don't think, do you, that the—the money may have come between them?" she said tentatively.

Astrea leaned forward to smooth away the frown with loving fingers.

"Perhaps," she said. "Marc admitted as much, but Roma, when she couldn't get him on her own terms, ran off with this American tycoon old enough to be her grandfather, and now he's dead and she has the dollars. No need for me to make a will in her favor."

"Is she not a relation, then?" Charity asked, wondering if Roma, like herself, had been one of the several companions.

"Not in blood, perhaps," Astrea replied dreamily. "In the spirit, I had thought—but no, our stars crossed. She is a Gemini, and they are notoriously uncertain and superficial and lazy at their lowest level. Roma's salvation would have been marriage with Marc, as I frequently told them both. He was born under Libra, you know, and that is the ideal harmonious partnership for Gemini subjects. You cannot go against the stars."

Charity sighed. How much havoc could a person of Astrea's temperament unwittingly create for others? she wondered. She had not liked Marc Gentle to any degree, but when she went up to bed that night she had the curiosity to look up the meaning of his sign in the pile of little books on the planets which Astrea had insisted on providing her with for study.

Libra, the Scales, she read with disgust. How appropriate and how chilly-sounding were all the attributes listed; logic, balance, detachment, love of justice . . . she was not surprised to read that Librans form few real friendships.

TWO WEEKENDS went by before Marc came to Cleat again, and when he did arrive he looked tired and on edge. Work had continued to pile up, he said; he had seldom left his chambers until late at night, and then worked on into the small hours at his flat and for most of the weekend.

"You should eat fruit and drink milk," his aunt told him sweepingly. "Librans should rule out all sugar, starch and heavy intoxicants."

He grinned at her tolerantly and helped himself to sherry.

"You shouldn't supply the intoxicants, in that case," he retorted. "How is the new companion shaping?"

"Oh, ideal, my dear boy, ideal! All those ridiculous forebodings of yours—quite wrong, of course. Why, she even told me I should consult you before changing my will."

He looked up sharply and his eyes narrowed.

"Astrea, you're not persisting in that folly, are you?" he said.

"What folly, dear boy?"

"You know very well. You've now suggested this absurd notion to the girl, I gather."

"Naturally. We have become very close. She has a most amazing gift for drawing my innermost thoughts from me."

"I don't doubt it," he countered dryly.

"And a born listener, my dear. Young, ignorant in many ways, as is only to be expected, but so gentle . . . so *simpatica . . .*"

"I'll bet she is!"

Astrea paused in her vague wanderings about the room and looked at her nephew with gathering petulance.

"Why have you taken against the child—a girl you know nothing about?" she asked.

He sipped his sherry thoughtfully. It was so like Astrea to explode her bombshells without thought to the propitiousness of the moment, he reflected wryly. He was in no mood to do battle with her after a gruelling three weeks of legal work.

"I haven't taken against her, as you put it," he answered a little wearily. "I can only point out, as I have on other occasions, that it's unwise to rush into these things without due consideration. Your lawyers will give you the same advice if you are foolish enough to consult them."

"I've already done so," she replied regally. "I have an appointment with old Mr. Fenimore for one day next week, and if you get in first and try to interfere, as you did once before, Cleat will not remain open house to you, Marc."

It was an old threat and empty with much repetition. She was, he knew, too fond of him to close the door in his face for long, but she was also a woman who thrived on opposition, and he had no wish to aggravate the situation. He must, he saw, tackle the girl. A few brutal home truths should put the fear of God into her.

"Fenimore can be trusted to look after your interests without my intervention," he said mildly.

"He cannot refuse to draw up a fresh will for me."

"No, he can't do that, but he can institute discreet enquiries and scare this little fortune-hunter off if you won't listen to sense."

"Really, Marc, you talk of the girl as if she were a trickster, a—a sort of *confidence* crook!" she exclaimed.

"It's tragic that a successful career at the Bar has only made you think the worst of your fellow creatures."

"Rather inevitable, I'm afraid, when one is a criminal lawyer."

"Charity is not like that. She was honest enough, as I told you, to suggest I consulted you, knowing you're a lawyer."

"Very astute of her," he murmured.

"I might even," announced his aunt triumphantly, "adopt her. Yes, that's what I'll do if there's any more trouble. I'll adopt her legally. She's still under age, so that would be much the best course."

It was an unfortunate moment for Charity to have to make her entrance before they all went into dinner. She had been long enough at Cleat House now to feel at her ease, even in renewing acquaintance with a man who had so plainly resented her, and she bore no one ill-will for long. Charity had a simple approach to life. She did not feel she would ever like Marc Gentle, but she could see his objection to his aunt's being exploited by strangers, and she was prepared to efface herself as much as possible during his visit. But as she shook hands with him, she was aware immediately of a fresh antagonism and her own dislike leapt instantly to meet it.

"Dear, dear Ganymede," Astrea said effusively, enveloping the girl in an extravagant embrace, largely, Charity suspected, to annoy her nephew. They had been having words, she thought unhappily, and, judging by the behavior of both, the argument had concerned herself.

Astrea was at her most provocative throughout the meal, bestowing unwelcome attentions upon Charity while she ignored Marc with pointed displeasure. Really, thought Charity helplessly, she's like a child! It was evident that Marc shared her sentiments, for he failed with admirable calm to respond to her jibes, and, although ob-

viously very tired, made an effort to keep some small talk
flowing to bridge the awkward gaps in the evening.

Back in the music-room Astrea demanded that Charity
should play some old *arias* for her as if they were still
alone, but Charity privately thought her employer had had
things her own way for too long. It was a little hard on the
disagreeable Mr. Gentle that he should continue to be subjected to such childishness when he looked as tired as he
did. She made an excuse that she had mending to do, and
went early to bed.

Whatever the reason for Astrea's behavior, by the next
morning her mood had entirely changed. She was full of
attentions towards her nephew, and, having bade him with
earnest solicitude to rest and relax and do nothing, promptly
insisted that he should drive her in to Brighton on one of
her exhausting shopping sprees.

Charity did not go with them. She had, so far, scarcely
had two words with Marc alone, and it would appear that
he seemed as anxious to avoid her company as she his. It
was, therefore, a complete surprise when on Sunday morning, as she was about to start out for a walk on the downs,
he announced his intention of coming with her.

"Oh!" she said blankly. She did not want his company
in the secret, solitary places she had found for herself,
neither could she imagine what they would find to talk
about.

"Do you object?" he enquired with raised eyebrows.

"No, of course not," she replied a little awkwardly, and
they set out together down the short drive and out on to the
chalk track which wound to the first breast of downland.

They did not talk very much, for the way to Cleat
Beacon was steep, and although Marc appeared unaffected
by the effort of climbing, Charity still felt the effects of
sedentary city life and arrived at the top breathless.

"You seem out of training," he observed as they paused

on the crest of the Beacon and she laughingly begged for a rest.

"Until I came here I had little chance for exercise," she said, and lifted her face to the sky, sniffing the strong air. "Up here there's always a wind. I love it."

He watched her thoughtfully, observing the unwonted color in her cheeks and the rather endearing disorder of her short dark hair. She wore a plain rough fisherman's jersey under a faded leather jerkin, and the black, tapered slacks made her legs look incredibly long. She seemed very young and very naive as she stood there with her face lifted to the wind, and he frowned. He was unused to dealing with twenty-year-olds except in the criminal courts, and this girl vaguely troubled him.

"I've got my breath now," she said, and they began to walk along the broad ridge of the Beacon. "How do you manage to keep fit, Mr. Gentle, living in London?"

"I play squash whenever I get the time," he answered absently. "What other jobs have you had?"

"Not many. Before I worked for the music publishers I had a job as typist in a firm of solicitors, but I got the sack."

"Oh, what for?" he asked, and she thought there was a ring of satisfaction in his voice.

"My speed wasn't good enough," she answered meekly, and was aware of the quick glance he gave her. "Well, before that I went out charring."

"Charring!"

"Yes, it's quite respectable, and you get very good pay by the hour. I don't mind housework."

"But surely there must have been more suitable ways of earning a living?"

"Not if you're untrained for anything. You see, it was the only way I could earn enough money to go to a commercial school in the evenings and learn to be a typist. And before I went out charring I was still at school—so you see—".

"I see."

She was either very ingenuous or she was speaking the plain truth. The reason for her dismissal could, of course, be checked with the firm of solicitors, but the likelihood of a young girl in her teens, who was clearly gently bred going out charring rather stuck in his throat. He glanced at her striding out resolutely beside him. The hair blew back from her face like a dark pennant and her ears were pink from the sting of the wind.

"I understand my aunt has suggested changing her will in your favor," he said conversationally. "Did you know she had made an appointment to see her lawyers next week?"

She looked up at him with evident surprise.

"No, I didn't," she said. "Your aunt mentioned something the other day, but I didn't take her seriously."

"No? Or the idea of adopting you?"

She looked even more surprised.

"She never said anything about that. Can one adopt grown-up people?"

"In the eyes of the law you are a minor until you are twenty-one."

"Oh! But I shouldn't think—I mean it doesn't seem very likely, does it?"

"You're very ingenuous, Charity Child," he said, and it was plain from his tone how he intended her to take his interpretation of her name.

She stopped abruptly and turned to face him.

"Are you suggesting that I—I've been getting at your aunt?" she asked, and the inconsequent gaiety had gone from her voice.

"Yes, I think perhaps I am. I've watched you playing up to her so innocently, feeding her vanity, falling in with this ridiculous spiritual daughter business. I think you're more dangerous than the other little gold-diggers from whose clutches I had to extricate her, so I'm warning you now.''

"Warning me?'' She sounded bewildered, and the hurt look of disbelief in her eyes made him speak harshly.

"Yes, warning you, my dear little girl. My aunt has had these quixotic notions before. She's easily won by flattery, as I've no doubt you've discovered for yourself, and a clever little nobody with an eye to the main chance could doubtless make a fairly easy killing, but I'll be watching you, Charity. Don't think for one moment you'll pull the wool over *my* eyes, for you won't get away with it.''

She hugged the leather jacket close to her body as if she felt suddenly cold.

"Do you want me to go?'' she asked bleakly, and he raised his eyebrows.

"Oh, no, that would make a martyr of you. You can stay as long as you behave yourself, for my aunt plainly doesn't share my doubts, but remember I'll be watching, and at the first sign of—shall we say undue influence—I'll have you out of Cleat in twenty-four hours. Now, do you understand?''

She had gone so white that he began to feel uneasy, and he was conscious that he had chosen his moment badly. Up here on the Beacon, with the wind blowing coldly, the scudding clouds and the loneliness, she could elude him. She no longer seemed the sort of person he accused her of being.

"I understand very well,'' she said. "I understand that you've resented and disliked me from the first.''

"Not disliked you. You have a way with you, Charity Child, I'll give you that.''

"I have no way with me—I've never learnt,'' she retorted coldly, then suddenly stamped her foot at him.

"You needn't be tolerant, Mr. Gentle,'' she cried. "I've

disliked you every bit as much! I may be a nobody, as you suggest, but I'm not used to suspicion—no, not even from the people I used to char for who might have been watching to see I didn't pinch the spoons! You must, I think, have had a very unfortunate experience of life."

He knew a quite irrational impulse to take her in his arms and either shake her or kiss her. She had, for all her youth and inexperience, a trick of getting under his skin. She was plain and immature, he thought angrily, suddenly remembering Roma, then as she continued to stand before him with the wind whipping the thin slacks against her long, slender legs, he reluctantly amended his opinion. She would never be entirely plain, he thought, with those great, fringed eyes and plaintive brows.

"Bravo!" he said, meeting her defiance with cynical appreciation. "Well, now we've both had our little say, shall we go back?"

"You can go back at your own pace—I've had enough," she said and, turning, began to run from him along the ridge of the Beacon. The wind was behind her and she was soon a diminishing figure in the distance as he stood and watched her. He paused to light a cigarette, then leisurely followed in her wake.

CHAPTER THREE

IT WAS difficult, Charity found, after he had gone back to London, to resume the old relationship with Astrea. She felt as awkward as a schoolgirl when her employer showered her with extravagant praise, but when she withdrew into herself, it was only to be met with reproach.

"What's the matter with you?" Astrea complained with brimming eyes. "We have been so close, dear child. What had made you stiff and unnatural—all that delightful spontaneity gone?"

Charity felt her own eyelids sting. She had grown very fond of Astrea in the short time she had been at Cleat, and it was hard to resist the first affection that had come her way since her father died.

"If you hadn't suggested changing your will—" she blurted out, and Astrea's eyes gleamed with sudden interest.

"Marc has been talking to you," she cried triumphantly. "You should pay no attention, child—my affairs have nothing whatever to do with him. I have changed my will before now, and will doubtless do it again."

"Yes, of course," Charity said, with a lifting heart.

This nonsense about the will and adoption was only one of the many foibles with which Astrea amused herself. Her nephew should have known that. But she went to London to consult her solicitors, for all that, taking Charity with her, and, when the interview was over, seemed in high spirits and took Charity shopping, spending money on her with reckless abandon, only saving on their lunch which they surprisingly had at an A.B.C. She did not tell the girl of the outcome of her visit to the lawyers, and Charity could not ask. This orgy of spending was, she suspected, embarked upon chiefly to annoy her nephew, for Astrea bade her wear her new clothes the following weekend, and when she did so a little reluctantly, repeatedly drew Marc's attention to every garment with an embarrassing exposition of how much each one had cost.

Once or twice Charity thought his eyes rested on her with a certain sympathy, but that weekend she seldom found herself alone with him, and the weekend after he remained in London.

Snow fell towards the end of February and lasted well into March. Charity delighted in the unbroken beauty of the white-clad downs and the wind that stung her face, but Astrea developed a bronchial cough and moped in her room with a blazing fire and all the windows shut.

"Such a country, such a climate!" She grumbled. "Here we are well into March, with Easter only three weeks off, and look at the weather! I never could stand the cold, it's always affected my voice."

"Why don't you spend your winters abroad?" asked Charity, thinking that with so much money at her disposal, Astrea made little use of the many opportunities that wealth must offer.

"No, no, I'm getting an old woman," she said fretfully. "When you are into the sixties, dear child, you cease wanting to roam."

"Seventy, if you're a day!" murmured Minnie, who was brushing her hair.

"Nonsense!" Astrea said sharply. "I'm sixty-seven, to be exact."

"That you're not!" Minnie retorted. "I'm sixty-nine meself, and you were always five years older, if not six."

"Go away, you're pulling my hair, you silly old woman!" Astrea said crossly. "And leave my heart medicine where I can reach it, this time."

"Heart medicine?" echoed Charity, startled, and Minnie gave one of her surprising Cockney winks.

"That's what she likes to call it," she sniffed. "Nothing but ipecacuanha, I shouldn't wonder."

"You know very well—" began Astrea, enraged, but the old dresser affected another wink, this time in her mistress's direction, and stumped out of the room.

When Marc came down at the end of the week, his aunt was still in bed and he glanced a little sharply at Charity's peaked face. She looked thinner, he thought, and that ridiculous resemblance to Pierrot was more marked.

"Haven't you been getting out?" he asked, and when she explained that she had been thoughtless in neglecting Astrea when the snow first came and was now making amends, he exclaimed: "Rubbish! Tomorrow we'll go for a long walk and pelt each other with snowballs."

She looked surprised, then dubious. She had no wish to repeat her only experience of walking with him, neither could she imagine the fastidious Marc Gentle throwing snowballs.

"You don't care for the notion?" he asked, looking amused.

"Not particularly."

"H'm . . ." he said, non-committally, but it would, she realized, be difficult to avoid his company this weekend. Apart from the fact that his mood seemed to have changed, they would, if Astrea remained in her room, be forced to eat solitary meals together, an intimacy Charity viewed with dismay. He would, she felt sure, return to the attack, and although of late Astrea had not mentioned the subject of her will, there had been letters and telephone calls from the solicitors, as much, Charity had thought, to relieve the boredom of a sick-room as anything else.

However, when they sat down alone to dinner, he indulged in the polite small talk he would have exerted on a strange and rather shy guest, surprising Charity with an easy charm she had not thought he possessed, and succeeding at last in loosening her own unwilling tongue.

"That's better!" he said when she laughed spontaneously at some mild quip. "I've seldom had to work so hard to put a girl at her ease."

She lowered her lashes and looked down at her plate.

"You can scarcely have expected me to feel at my ease with you, Mr. Gentle," she replied. Astrea had long ago insisted that her nephew should be addressed by his Christian name, but Charity had found it a difficult habit to acquire.

He grinned a little wryly.

"Perhaps not," he said. "Perhaps I was altogether too hasty in my original judgment."

She looked enquiringly across at him in the candlelight. The expression on his dark face was quizzical and even conciliatory.

"Is that meant for a—an apology?" she asked, stammering slightly.

"If you like. I don't withdraw everything, mind you, but you are not, I've discovered, the sort of young person I took you to be."

"You've been making enquiries, perhaps?"

"Naturally. Your firm of solicitors gave you a good character, so did the commercial school. They had, they said, never before had so young a pupil who had gone out charring."

"Well, *really*!" Charity exclaimed, not sure whether to be relieved or outraged that he had seen fit to investigate her statements.

His eyes surprisingly twinkled.

"You've no great liking for me, have you, Charity?" he said.

"You've hardly set out to inspire that," she retorted.

He observed her thoughtfully, annoyed that he should

care one way or the other whether she liked him or not.

"You must blame it on my court-room manner," he said lightly. "Well, shall we call a truce?"

"Legal questions are one of the worries of Aquarians," she told him sedately, and he gave a sharp exclamation of impatience.

"For heaven's sake! You're not becoming infected with my aunt's obsession with the stars, are you?" he said.

"The books she has lent me are very interesting," she replied demurely.

"I don't doubt it. And what are the other worries of Aquarians?"

"Situations of mental strain, lack of appreciation of efforts—among others."

"I see."

Was she getting at him, he wondered, giving her a searching glance. She had side-stepped neatly, he noticed, his offer of a truce, and her cool indifference began to irritate him.

"Well, my dear," he observed with deliberate indifference, "it makes no odds if you choose to bear malice. I only thought it might prove easier if we met on a civilized basis, since we will see a good deal of one another."

She sat considering this, fiddling with the cutlery beside her plate. He was not to know, she supposed, how harsh he could sound, or how easily he could charm, if he chose.

"I don't think I ever bear malice," she said. "If I have been rude to you, Mr. Gentle, it was only you who drove me to it. You're not, after all, my employer."

"Very true," he replied crisply. "But you'd better acquire the habit of my Christian name or you'll annoy my aunt."

"I'm sorry. I find it difficult to think of you as Marc."

"Because you don't like me? Really, Charity Child, you're a most irritatingly self-possessed young woman!"

Charity was relieved that Minnie chose that moment to bring in the next course. She did not feel self-possessed at all; indeed, this change of front in him was as alarming as his early suspicions. He could make her feel gauche and tongue-tied more easily in his present mood than when he was accusing her of unspeakable things. He was, she thought, a very uncomfortable person to live with, whatever his intention.

The silence grew when Minnie had left the room. Charity could think of nothing to say, and Marc, it seemed, had no inclination to return to his earlier rôle of attentive host. They ate in silence at Astrea's well-appointed table, and outside the wind began to rise. It had almost reached gale force by the time they returned to the music-room, and Marc drew back the curtains to reveal the snow driven with blinding fury against the window.

"It looks as if we're in for the blizzard they've been having in the north," he observed.

"Will we be snowbound?" Charity asked watching, with awe, a sight she had never before beheld.

"It has happened up here on the downs," he answered. "Were you fearing you might have to put up with my company for longer than a weekend?"

"No," she said. "I was thinking of the lambs."

"The lambs?"

"Yes. There are new-born lambs on the downs. How will they survive? How will they find their mothers?"

There was suddenly such anguish in her voice that he placed gentle hands on her shoulders and turned her round to face him.

"The farmers and shepherds will see to them," he said. "What a strange child you are, Charity—does suffering move you so much?"

"Of course," she said simply, but her grave eyes told him that she could not expect him to share her compassion.

He let her go and drew the curtains across the window again.

"Will you do something for me?" he asked. "Will you play *Au clair de la lune* for me again?"

She did not refuse, although she was made wary by his request, but went at once to the piano and began to play. The gentle melody was almost drowned by the force of the wind and when she had finished she asked:

"Why did you ask for that?"

He lay back in his chair, his eyes still intent upon her.

"Perhaps because it describes you," he replied lazily.

"But the first time you thought I'd chosen it on purpose—to play up to your aunt," she said baldly, and he got up impatiently and stood with his back to the fire, looking down at her.

"Are you always going to hark back to my possible misconception of your motives?" he demanded irascibly.

"You made it difficult for me to forget," she replied, her hands still resting idly on the keyboard. "I think, perhaps, you've become too used to bullying defenceless witnesses."

His expression was a little grim.

"All right," he said. "If you want to quarrel with me, you shall. You're like all your sex; you never can let a thing alone. If I harbored suspicions of you it was for a very good reason, and I'm not sure now that you aren't being just a shade more subtle than your predecessors. You're intelligent enough to have summed up my aunt's character and your own chances at the very first meeting. You hardly expected someone like myself to throw a wrench into the works, did you?"

"Oh!" she cried, springing to her feet. "You're disgusting and—and unbearable! I'll go away . . . I'll go this minute!"

She was across the room and out of the door before he could speak. A moment later he heard the front door slam, and with a muttered profanity, he went after her.

The icy wind lashed at him, and at first he could see nothing in the blinding snow. He shouted, but his voice was carried away by the wind and he began to stagger with difficulty down the drive. He found her very quickly, shivering and crying in the snowdrift into which she had fallen. He picked her up and carried her back to the house and set her urgently on her feet in front of the fire.

"Well!" he observed grimly. "How far did you imagine you'd get on a night like this, without even stopping for a coat, let alone your luggage?"

"I don't know . . . I didn't think . . . I just had to get away from you. . . ." She spoke incoherently and a little wildly, the self-possession which had annoyed him completely gone. She stood before him wet and weeping, and the snowflakes melted in small rivulets on her hair and frock.

He knelt beside her and began to chafe her cold hands, experienced that old, irrational impulse to shake or kiss her. But the anger had gone from him and something very like tenderness took its place.

"You foolish child!" he said gently. "Don't you realize you sometimes goad me into these unkind speeches?"

"No?" she said "Why?"

"I don't know. Perhaps I'm not used to such coolness in the average witness."

"But why do you treat me like a witness at all? I—I've done nothing wrong."

"No, I don't think you have. Well, shall we try to forget this unfortunate start to our friendship?"

"Friendship?"

"I'd like to think so. Indeed there is a great deal I'd like to discover about you, Charity Child."

She politely released her hands from his and began to rub away the tears.

"I'll try to forget it, Mr. Gentle—Marc, I mean," she said shyly. "I told you I don't bear malice."

"No, I don't think you would," he said, getting to his feet. "Now, we'd both better dry out by the fire and get acquainted. If your worst fears are realized and we find ourselves snowbound tomorrow, we can't spend the days bickering, can we?"

For the first time she began to like him. His disordered
hair gave him a faintly raffish appearance and the legs of
his trousers, wet from the deep snow he had walked
through had lost their immaculate crease.

"I'm sorry for giving you trouble," she said, and added
with a slow, unexpected grin: "You almost look
disreputable—I like it much better."

THEY WERE not, however, snowbound. By the morning the
blizzard had blown itself out. Snow had piled up in great
drifts during the night, but the snow ploughs were out on
the roads and although the tradesmen's vans could not
reach Cleat on account of the icy hill, a thaw was forecast
for Sunday.

Marc surprised Charity by dealing efficiently and
knowledgeably with frozen pipes and blocked plumbing
and, assisted by Charity, cleared a path from the house to
the drive gates.

He seemed to be enjoying himself, and Charity, shovelling away beside him until her back ached, experienced the
first sense of pleasure she had known in his company.

Every so often, she would lean on her shovel and gaze a
little wistfully at the curving line of the downs, and Marc
said, with unexpected perception:

"Still thinking of those lambs?"

"Yes," she said, "they worry me."

"Don't let them. There are very few losses these days.
Do you know that poem of Robert Bridges that begins:

> *'I never shall love the snow again
> Since Maurice died?'* "

"No. Is it about lambs?"

"No, but I suppose you started a connection for me between snow and sadness . . .

> *'They brought him home, 'twas two days late
> For Christmas Day . . .' "*

It seemed strange to hear him quoting poetry as if he loved it. She had not thought that he would have found time for the solitary delights of verse.

"Do you read much poetry?" she enquired.

"Oh, yes. But I come of an older generation than yours," he replied.

"But I read poetry, too," she said shyly. "My father used to read aloud to me."

"You speak as though you still miss him. Tell me about yourself, Charity."

"There's nothing much to tell. My father and I were very close to one another. He was, I suppose, rather a failure in life, for he never made much money with his music, but we didn't mind."

"And your mother?"

"She died when I was very small. I don't remember her."

"I see," he said gently, and began shovelling again. "And your father died after you had left school?"

"During my last term."

The scrape of Marc's shovel suddenly reminded her vividly of the tiny, unrewarding garden her father had tended so hopefully in the last home they had shared, and she cried, with unfamiliar resentment:

"It was so unfair! I'd been counting the days till I could come home and keep house for him, and I never had the chance. I don't think he really got enough to eat, except in the holidays. I only realized afterwards how he must have scrimped and saved in order to educate me."

"Had you no other relatives?"

"No. Father was an only child, like me, and my mother's family emigrated to New Zealand years and years ago. I don't even know if they are still alive."

"We have something in common, after all," he said prosaically. "Astrea is my only living relative, and when my mother died, I missed her as much as you have missed your father."

"Did you?" she said softly, and watched him shovelling the snow with a fresh perception.

He looked up and saw her watching him. Her eyes seemed solemn and faintly troubled, like the grave eyes of a puzzled child. She was, he realized with amused surprise, weighing him up and assessing what she found.

"What are you thinking about?" he asked. "Not those lambs again, I hope."

"No," she answered politely. "But my thoughts were private."

He suddenly threw down his shovel, and scooping up handfuls of snow, began to pelt her with it. For a moment she was too surprised to do anything but stand and stare, then as a well-aimed snowball caught her full on the chest, she began to retaliate. They pelted each other like a couple of children until Charity fell down and had to be pulled, laughing, from a snowdrift; then they looked towards the house at the sound of a peremptory tapping, to see Astrea standing at the window of her room with Minnie's little wizened face peering over her shoulder. Astrea clasped her hands and nodded and made extravagant gestures of approval, but Minnie, when they went indoors to change their wet clothes, remarked:

"*Reely,* Mr. Marc—at *your* age!"

Astrea joined them later in the day, tired of her self-imposed solitude. She was draped in an ancient tea-gown and several layers of shawls, and her hair badly needed retouching.

"I'm missing all the fun," she said, adding, as she saw her nephew's glance at her hair: "I know, I know, dear boy—you needn't look down your long nose. My roots are terrible, and so *grey!* Charity must do them, for I won't be able to get to my hairdresser in this weather. Charity, dear child, we will have a *session* with the hair-dye tomorrow. I always keep some handy.''

"Oh, Astrea, I wouldn't dare!" exclaimed Charity, thoroughly alarmed. "I've no experience of tinting hair. I might do something awful!"

"Nonsense!" Astrea cried, dismissing the matter. "You just mix and dab and mix and dab. Minnie often does it."

"Why don't you let it grow grey?" Marc enquired with lazy amusement.

"Because, as you know very well, it expresses my personality," snapped his aunt. "Red—gold—yellow—all the colors of the Star-maiden. I was famed for my hair as well as my voice, you know—now, my hair is all that is left to me."

It was one of her unconscious moments of pathos, and Charity looked at her fondly. She had often wondered how much aching nostalgia lay under the histrionics and pose of eccentricity; another lonely person, perhaps, shut up in an ivory tower.

"You have your records, Astrea," she said gently. "Your voice will never die."

"Yes, yes, that's true. Singers of today have lost what we had—the grand presence, the temperament—royal personages following one around incognito."

"No royal how-d'-you-dos followed you around, duck, to my certain knowledge," observed Minnie, entering that moment with the tea. It still surprised Charity when the old dresser lapsed into the familiar speech of the theatre.

"How do you know, if they were travelling incognito?" demanded Astrea reasonably.

Marc, used to these altercations, smiled his enjoyment, and Minnie set the tray down before Charity, whose duty it was to pour out, and retorted flatly:

"If that's your way of saying they wasn't there, then you're right. Now, keep those shawls fastened your first day downstairs. You aren't no chicken any more."

"Really, Minnie is becoming impossible!" Astrea exclaimed as the door closed again. "Now, tell me about yourselves, my dears. I couldn't believe my *eyes* when I saw you snowballing this morning—so uninhibited, so healthy! You have called a truce, yes?"

Marc's eyes twinkled.

"My offers of a truce weren't very kindly received last night," he said, and Charity picked up the teapot quickly, spilling the tea in her haste to avoid his glance.

"Well, I've no doubt you confused the child with your legal twists and traps," said Astrea calmly. "All the same, dear Charity, you must try to come to terms with my nephew. I have a little scheme which was born when I watched you this morning. I looked it all up to be quite sure. Libra and Aquarius form a perfect Harmonious Grouping."

Charity, who was not paying much attention, had little idea of what Astrea was hinting, but Marc evidently had. His eyes narrowed, and for a moment the indulgent amusement went out of his face, leaving it cold and shuttered.

"Keep your little schemes in check, my dear aunt," he said. "They can't concern me any longer."

"Why not?"

He smiled then, aware of Charity's unblinking gaze.

"You can play your hand once too often," he said enigmatically. "Besides, you may put the poor girl off me again. I'm not entirely in her good graces yet, you know."

The look which Astrea bestowed on them both was so frankly arch that Charity felt uncomfortable.

"That's scarcely surprising, since you made no bones about it that you thought she was after my money," she retorted, her mouth full of tea-cake. "I trust you've revised your opinion, dear boy?"

"Trust—yes, that's the crux of the matters, isn't it, Astrea? But we're embarrassing Charity."

They were, indeed, embarrassing her, talking as if she wasn't there at all, and Marc, for all his allusions to a truce, was as ambiguous in his comments as ever.

"Never be embarrassed, dear child," said Astrea before she could speak. "Only the mediocre, the *bourgeois* are that. Me, I was able to carry off any situation—but *any* situation with superb aplomb."

"Dear Astrea, I'm sure you could," Charity said, her embarrassment vanishing in laughter. Astrea, although given to the most devastating personalities, could also be relied upon to relieve an awkward moment with some extravagance.

Astrea passed her cup for some more tea.

"And now, Marc, what about the Easter Vacation? Are you coming here, or are you going to walk?" she asked.

"Walking means a species of climbing, or rather scrambling, in the Welsh hills or the Lake District," he explained, seeing Charity's look of surprise. "I'd like to come here, I think, if you'll have me, Astrea."

Charity was aware that he gave her a rather sardonic glance of amusement as he spoke, but his aunt clapped her hands in delight.

"Well, isn't that nice!" she exclaimed. "You and dear Charity can really get acquainted, and you will put your car at my disposal, will you not, dear boy?"

"It's always at your disposal, Astrea."

"Yes, of course, but sometimes you get a little *bored*, I think. Still, it saves Skinners' bills, and that is most important."

Charity supposed that Astrea, with all her money, could well have afforded to keep a car and a chauffeur, but it was another of her eccentricities that she preferred to hire both car and driver from the village and otherwise rely on her friends for transport.

"It seems ridiculous preparing for Easter when we are surrounded by snow and ice," she said. "Charity, dear child, run upstairs and fetch me another shawl—the embroidered silk which the Spanish ambassador sent to the Opera House the night I sang Tosca—I'm not sure where it is, but Minnie will know."

Charity suspected that this was one of Astrea's transparent manoeuvres to get her out of the room and, indeed, as soon as the door had closed behind her, Astrea turned cosily to her nephew.

"*Now,* Marc—what have you to tell me?" she said.

"Why, nothing," he replied, with raised eyebrows.

"Oh, don't be so irritating! I want to know what you think of my little Ganymede, now that you've had her to yourself. My scheme perhaps was born before today."

"Once and for all, Astrea, forget about your schemes," he said quietly. "You often think up these fantasies to relieve your own boredom, I know, but Roma should have been a lesson to you."

"Ah, Roma! But you were in agreement with me there."

"Yes, and it was I who got hurt. It doesn't do to play providence."

"It was a bitter hurt to me, too, dear boy. I wonder how she is wearing her widowhood. Weeds should become her."

"Widows don't wear weeds, these days," he commented dryly. "And I've no doubt the Nixon dollars will help to ease her bereavement."

"How bitter you sound," she said. "You have never quite got her out of your system, have you?"

"Oh, I think so. How are you progressing with your plans for adoption?" He had switched the subject so abruptly that she had no time to dissemble with her usual skill.

"Mr. Fenimore has everything in hand," she answered a little sulkily. "I wonder you haven't made it your business to find out."

"Oh, I have. Fenimore is no more approving than I am, as I think he's told you. Has he drawn up a will?"

"If he has, it's my affair. You can only withdraw your objections now, dear boy, since you've altered your opinions of my spiritual daughter."

"Did I say I had?" he countered smoothly, and, for one moment, she looked taken aback.

"But I thought—well, this weekend—"

"Don't meddle, Astrea," he told her with sudden sternness. "Whether you carry out this hare-brained notion is, as you say, ultimately your affair, but don't meddle in other matters."

"Such as?"

"You know very well. A point of view that seems to have escaped you is the girl's position if you make her your heiress. Do you want her to be married for her expectations?"

"Well, it would be better than not being married at all," his aunt replied with her usual frankness, and his eyebrows rose.

"You don't seem to have a very flattering opinion of your protégée's powers of attraction," he observed mildly, and she began wildly retrieving her slipping shawls catching her rings and her charms in the wool, in a sudden fever of exasperation.

"Of *course* I have!" she protested. "A dear child, a *kind* child—so like poor Pierrot—but plain, perhaps, do you think?"

"No."

"No? You do surprise me, dear boy. When one thinks of Roma . . ."

"That's your trouble, isn't it, my dear?" he said gently. "You still hanker after Roma, and Charity is just the standin."

"No, no, they are quite different," Astrea cried. "Roma disappointed me bitterly and I no longer want her back. This dear child fills all the corners of my heart."

"So did the others," he reminded her with sudden dryness. "They were all figure heads for Roma, whether you realized it or not, but this dear child, as you call her now, could be hurt when you tire of her."

His aunt got up and began to prowl about the room as

she always did in moments of agitation, and the multitudes of little charms jangled merrily as she gesticulated.

"I don't know what's got into you, Marc," she exclaimed. "First you say the girl is out for what she can get and I'm a gullible old fool, and next you are only concerned with *her* feelings, and not at all with *mine*. Why should I tire of her? Is she not associated with Ganymede, the Cup-bearer, and am I not planning a future for the child—the future that should have been Roma's?"

He uttered a short, sharp sigh of defeat. As a witness, he thought wryly, his aunt might well baffle the most astute cross-examiner; her logic was negligible and her statements quite unpredictable.

"Have it your own way, my dear," he said with a tired smile. "You usually do, if it comes to that."

THE THAW started in the night, and all Sunday the miracle of whiteness lost its beauty, leaving behind slush and mud and battered fences.

All the morning Charity had battled with Astrea's hair-dye. It had been a formidable experience, for Astrea, never patient with other people's ineptness, had directed proceedings with alarming thoroughness and frequent abuse. Charity sat down to luncheon with heavily stained fingers, and Marc, glancing at her worried face, said, with a brief smile:

"Is this your first experience of Astrea's tantrums? You'll have to get used to it, you know, if you want to stay."

"It was all rather unnerving," she admitted, looking ruefully at her stained hands. "I was terrified her hair would go green, or something. Dyes *can* go wrong, can't they?"

"I imagine so. Why on earth didn't you wear rubber gloves? That stuff will take days to come off." He spoke a little sharply, and she hastily hid her hands under the table, remembering how fastidious he always seemed about his own person.

"No one suggested it," she answered nervously. "Minnie was annoyed, I think, at your aunt insisting I did the job, and just stood there glumly and wouldn't help."

"Poor Charity! Playing spiritual daughter to a temperamental prima donna isn't all beer and skittles, is it?" he observed, and she thought the old mockery was back in his voice and the glances he occasionally gave her not too kindly. Did he, like Minnie, resent his aunt's attachment for her, she wondered wistfully, but when, later, they sat by the fire in the music-room listening to the steady drip of the thaw and the dull thuds of lumps of snow falling off the roof, he asked her suddenly if she would like him to read to her.

She acquiesced with gratitude for the return of a side of his personality which she was beginning to like, and curled pleasurably up on the rug to listen. He read her poems from *A Shropshire Lad*, which her father had loved, and the poem he had quoted from in the snow, yesterday. He read well, without the affectations of many readers of verse, and she thought he must often read aloud to himself for the sheer delight of speaking the lines.

"Yes, I do," he admitted with a smile when she asked him. "Poetry, I think, needs not be spoken aloud for full appreciation."

"That's what my father used to say. What secret, solitary sort of things you do!"

His eyebrows rose.

"Such as?"

"Well, this, and climbing mountains—scrambling, didn't you call it? What else?"

"Sometimes I go abroad and wander round the art galleries, sometimes I explore forgotten corners of the British Isles and just mooch."

"Always alone?"

"Yes."

She sighed.

"Loneliness can be a little sad, can't it?" she said.

"I haven't found it so," he replied.

"But your kind of loneliness is self-imposed," she said shrewdly. "It can be different when it's thrust upon you."

He looked at her with gentleness.

"And have you found that, Charity?" he asked, watching her pale, unawakened face in the firelight.

"In a way, I suppose. I don't make friends easily, you see," she answered simply. "The girls I met at work only wanted to talk about clothes and boys. They all had boys, of course."

"And was there no boy for you?"

"Oh, no, they found me dull. I expect I was. I don't dance very well and don't care much for most of their interests. After my father's company they seemed very callow to me."

"Very likely, considering your father was a mature man," he retorted a little dryly. "You will probably always appeal more to an older man."

"Will I?" She sounded doubtful, as if the thought that she could appeal to any man was new to her.

"Don't you ever think about getting married, having a home of your own?" he asked curiously, and she shook her head.

"Not really—only as an imaginary picture of security," she said.

"Are you happy here? Does my aunt represent your notion of security?"

She considered this for some minutes, and he had noticed before how she seldom gave a hasty answer to a serious question.

"Yes," she said then. "Because she has an abundance to give and receive—not material things, I don't mean, and these fancies about adoption and legacies. You knew they were fancies, didn't you?"

"Yes, but I wondered if you did," he answered a shade austerely. "Astrea will hurt you, Charity."

"Hurt me? Oh, no! She's old and lonely and forgotten, and grateful for someone who really cares that she once was famous. Her tantrums, as you called them, won't hurt me, for I think she is fond of me, and I—well, I'm truly fond of her."

"I see," he said and, for a moment, felt angry with Astrea, whose affections were notoriously fickle. He had not, himself, contributed anything but harshness to this strange girl's conception of security, but at least he had not offered illusions which could be shattered by a passing whim.

He leaned forward into the circle of firelight and took her chin between finger and thumb, turning her face up to his.

"Be wary, my dear," he said. "Adoption might, I think, be difficult at this stage, but Astrea may well alter her will. If she does, you must remember that it can, as easily, be altered again. Don't build on shifting sand."

She did not understand him. He was, she supposed, trying to warn her, but he no longer seemed to be questioning her own motives.

"I wouldn't want the money, anyway," she said, trying to reassure him, "but the thought has a kind of comfort—that a stranger should love you enough to want to adopt you and leave you their money, I mean."

He leaned back in his chair a shade impatiently, and opened the book of verse on his knee.

"You'll have to dree your own weird, as they say in Scotland, Charity Child," he said with rough tolerance. "You are, I'm beginning to suspect, marked out for disappointment, disillusionment, and, probably, grief. You had no business to get yourself born into this day and age."

He began to read aloud again, and she sat watching the firelight play across his dark face, and knew a curious impulse to be friends with him, to be admitted to the closed circle of his solitariness and find her niche there. He was, she thought with surprise, a highly sensitive person under that professional mask he wore so well.

The house seemed empty after he had gone, and Charity, used all her life to a man's company, found she missed him. It was pleasant to look forward to the Easter Vacation when spring would surely have come to Cleat, and they would walk on the downs among the lambs and watch the miracle of tender shoots pushing up through the soil. Even by the end of the week the last traces of winter had gone. March has slipped into April with the gentleness of the proverb and the young grass was green with the promise of spring.

When Marc came at the weekend, he brought a present for Charity. It was only a cheap anthology of verse he had picked up at a second-hand bookstall in an idle moment, but for Charity, perhaps because it was so unexpected to receive a gift from him, it had an odd significance.

"For heaven's sake!" he exclaimed, momentarily irritated by her extravagant thanks. "Don't carry on as if I've spent a fortune on you—the thing isn't even new!"

"That doesn't matter," she said shyly, then stood there, dumb and ill at ease, conscious that she had been over-effusive.

Astrea's old eyes lit up with a naughty light when she was shown Marc's present, but almost at once she handed the book back with a snort of disgust.

"Second-hand!" she exclaimed. "But Marc always did like pottering about these musty old shops."

"My father used to say you sometimes picked up a treasure that way. Nearly all our books were second-hand. We couldn't afford new ones," Charity said.

"Well, Marc can," his aunt retorted. "I shall speak to him. This is not the way to start his courting."

"Courting?" For a moment Charity stared at her, open-mouthed, then she burst out laughing. "Astrea! What wild notion have you got up your sleeve now?"

"Just a little scheme I had, dear child. You like Marc, don't you?"

"I don't know him very well."

"That shall be remedied when he comes for his vacation. Marc ought to settle down. I've been saying so for years."

"Please—" began Charity with an alarming vision of how awkward such ludicrous manoeuvres could become, but Astrea waved her protestations aside.

"You know nothing of life," she proclaimed sweepingly. "Doubtless you are too ignorant and unsophisticated for someone like my nephew, but if I make you my heiress, things will be altogether different, won't they?"

"Not in the least—it wouldn't alter *me*," replied Charity rather shortly, remembering Roma, and Astrea swooped on her with one of the sudden enveloping embraces that put an end to all argument.

"Ah, my little Ganymede, *nothing* could alter you!" she cried. "You are my spiritual daughter—better, perhaps, to remain that way. Marc, too, should stay detached—celibate, would you say?"

"I really don't know," Charity replied a little breathlessly. It was profitless to try to follow Astrea's contradictory fancies, she decided ruefully, and at least Marc should understand his aunt by now, but the weekend was hardly restful.

Friday evening was spent in an orgy of record-playing. Astrea always insisted that the gramophone should be turned up full blast for opera, and the robust voices of the singers screaming above the Wagnerian brass echoed round the room until Charity's ears sang. Marc lay back in his chair, enduring with admirable detachment; it must, she thought, be torture for the uninitiated to be deafened by such a cacophony of sound. His eyes were closed and he only opened them to suggest that Charity should play them something soothing on the piano.

"Philistine!" said Astrea scornfully. "Such magnificent passion! Such great voices! Though I always say the soprano sings flat in that superb passage at the end. Now when I was at my height—''

"But you never aspired to Wagner, did you, Astrea?" her nephew reminded her unkindly. It was an admission which she never cared to make, for were not those in the top flight more famous for their exacting roles in German Grand Opera?

"Wagner is ruination to a more delicate voice, as you should know," she snapped. "Give him *Clair de lune*, Charity, hackneyed, sweet soothing syrup."

Charity went to the piano and the soft, plaintive music of Debussy's charming piece filled the room with a nostalgic quiet, and at the close, Astrea's mood had changed again.

"Charming . . . charming . . ." she sighed. "Moonlight . . . Pierrot . . . they both become the child, do they not, Marc?"

He made no reply, but only smiled a little enigmatically, and soon afterwards went to bed.

In the morning Astrea broke her rule of breakfasting in her room and dragged her nephew off to drive her round the countryside looking for a Home Craft colony newly settled in the district. They returned very late for lunch, cluttered with lengths of tweeds, shapeless jumpers and pottery of hideous design. Everything had to be displayed while Minnie grumbled in the background and declared the lunch to be ruined, and was not at all pacified by the gift of a jumper and a particularly ugly flower-vase.

"What on earth can you want with all this rubbish?" Marc asked impatiently. He had driven miles out of his way, following his aunt's vague directions, and had spent a wretched morning listening to Astrea trying to impress a dreary collection of amateur craftsmen who had clearly never heard of her.

"Well, one had to buy something, hadn't one?" she answered, and he grinned. Astrea had been very rude in her efforts to persuade the colony what an honor she was conferring upon them. Her purchases were, presumably, in the nature of a peace offering.

"After luncheon," she announced ominously, "we will *all* weed the garden. I cannot think what Noakes does with his time—weeds are sprouting *everywhere*. You and Charity—"

"No, my dear aunt, Charity and I are going for a quiet walk on the downs," Marc interrupted firmly. "I need a little quiet and meditation before offering myself for the noisy pleasures of the music-room."

"Perhaps the child will not want to walk," said Astrea petulantly.

"The child will," Marc replied, and did not seem to think it necessary to consult Charity.

"Wouldn't you like to get away on your own?" Charity asked him as they began to climb the chalk track which led to Cleat Beacon.

"Not particularly," he said, but they walked in silence for the most part, and Charity wondered if, amongst the trials of the morning, he had been subjected to his aunt's views on his future.

They walked along the ridge of the Beacon, and Charity remembered that other occasion when he had castigated her so cruelly and ruined a perfect day.

"Was this the spot?" he asked her suddenly.

She looked enquiringly, but was silent, still not sure of his mood.

"Where I bit you so badly. Isn't that what you were thinking of?" he said.

"You were unkind and very rude," she told him, lifting her face to the wind as he remembered her doing before. "You called me a gold-digger and a clever little nobody with an eye to the main chance. You warned me that you would have no hesitation in getting me out of Cleat if I—if I didn't behave myself."

"I'm glad to learn you have such a retentive memory," he observed mildly. "Perhaps I can match it. You told me you disliked me intensely and that I must have had a very unfortunate experience of life.''

''We would seem to be quits, then,'' she said demurely, and he put a hand for an instant on her shoulder.

''All the same, I should like to apologize,'' he said unexpectedly. ''I must have hurt you. I didn't, you see, understand much about you, then.''

''You sound as if it had worried you.''

''It has a bit. Your composure used to nettle me in those early days, I'll admit, but I hadn't realized how vulnerable you are.''

''Vulnerable?''

''I think so. You must remind me of that first occasion if I bite you again—and I probably will.''

''Because I'm ignorant and—and unsophisticated?''

''Why do you ask that?''

''Something your aunt said.''

The ready frown drew his dark eyebrows together.

''You don't take all my aunt's nonsense seriously, I hope,'' he said with a hint of displeasure, and she felt embarrassed, guessing that Astrea had, indeed, been meddling once again, and he was warning her.

''Of course not,'' she said hurriedly, side-stepping into the tufty grass, deliberately widening the space between them. ''You don't have to—have to fear complications from me, Marc.''

He closed the gap with one stride, and she was again conscious of his shoulder touching hers, and the queer intimacy of their solitude on that lonely strip of downland.

''Don't I?'' he said softly. ''But perhaps it won't be you who causes the complications. I think you are a new experience for me, Charity Child.''

''And you for me,'' she said, but did not sound too sure she liked it. He spoke, she thought, in riddles, as he so often did.

''You, my child, have no experience at all, thank heavens!'' he retorted calmly. ''Look! There are some of your lambs—none the worse, as you can see, for the blizzard. Do you know that old street cry:

> 'Young lambs to sell, white lambs to sell;
> If I'd as much money as I could tell
> I wouldn't be crying Young Lambs to sell!''

They turned back along the Beacon for home, and Charity felt release from her earlier doubts. They were the good companions of untroubled days, just as she and her father had been, striding over the springy turf in the wind, quoting snatches of poetry to one another-and old nursery rhymes.

When they came to the house, she was instantly reminded of her first arrival at Cleat, for the door swung open and there was Astrea in the porch, her arms outstretched to receive them.

"Such news, my dears!" she cried. "Such tremendous tidings! Roma is coming home and she wants to come *here*!"

CHAPTER FOUR

THERE WAS no music that evening, but Charity found the perpetual arguments exhausting. They discussed it endlessly, it seemed, at least Astrea did, returning again and again to opposing points of view, while Marc listened patiently.

Roma Nixon had cabled from America, apparently; she was sailing shortly and would arrive in time for Easter. Might she come home to her dear Astrea?

"So typical, so imaginative—the prodigal returning at Eastertide!" Astrea had said, the tears running down her cheeks, but almost in the next breath she had exclaimed: "I will *not* have her here! With all that money, she can well afford hotels. She ran away to marry that old man, leaving me alone—and you too, Marc—why should I welcome her now?"

And so it went on through the rest of the day and most of Sunday. One moment Roma was the spiritual daughter without whom Astrea could not exist, the next Charity had taken her place and a reunion with old ties was not to be thought of. At last, when at luncheon on Sunday Astrea turned to her nephew for the hundredth time to demand his advice, he replied with the taut irritability of a man whose patience was exhausted:

"Why ask me, for heaven's sake? You know perfectly well that you're enjoying every minute of this quite unnecessary disturbance, Astrea, and in the end you'll do exactly as you please. None of this can be very pleasant for Charity, who might well be excused for thinking herself in danger of the push in favor of Roma. We've both played up to you long enough. Now, for goodness' sake, drop it."

Astrea's eyes filled and she sent Charity a conciliatory look and a vague wave of the hand.

"But of *course* my little Ganymede wouldn't be sent away, should Roma come here," she said with plaintive reproach. "She is *simpatica*, which Roma often was not—this lamb is very tough, I believe it's mutton, Minnie must speak to the butcher—no, Charity, my dear, dear child, do not be anxious. After all, Roma would only be here on a visit, would she not?"

"So I imagine," Marc said shortly. "So what all the fuss is about, I can't think."

"You have forgotten, perhaps, how she treated me?"

"No, I haven't forgotten. When you made certain conditions in your will which I could not agree to, the girl took a short cut to wealth and security, and I, for one, couldn't blame her."

Astrea, who had long ago abandoned her diet of nuts, absently poured custard on to her meat in mistake for mint sauce and gazed at him with mournful eyes.

"I had forgotten your own feelings were involved, dear boy," she said in a muted tone. "You would not, of course, wish to come here for Easter if it meant meeting poor Roma again. How very thoughtless of your old aunt."

Charity had become accustomed to Astrea's disregard for the privacy of personal matters in front of other people, but she had been surprised that even Astrea had been able to ignore her nephew's reactions until this moment. When the news had first been broken to him his face had set into that cold mask of reserve which he had learnt so well to affect, and Charity thought there had been a brief but instantly suppressed hint of pain in his eyes, but now he merely regarded his aunt with a quizzical expression and retorted:

"My feelings are not involved at all, my dear aunt, so leave them out of your calculations."

"Then you would still come for Easter?"

"Naturally. I've no wish to upset my arrangements now."

"I wonder—" Astrea began reflectively, and Charity knew, as if the sentence had been completed, that another little scheme had just been born. Marc evidently knew it, too, for his smile was bitter and without amusement as he said:

"Make what arrangements you like, Astrea, but be warned by past experience. Seven years is a long time, and people change."

"I do not change ever, for I am Astrea, the Star-maiden—what a peculiar flavor," his aunt said absently, taking a mouthful of meat and custard. "Yes, dear boy, you are right. I must make the decision."

"Well, do it quickly, and then you can send off this wretched cable and we may be allowed to forget the whole thing for the rest of the day."

Astrea looked surprised.

"But I've already sent it. I sent it yesterday, before you got home. The stars were most propitious."

Marc who had been about to drink his accustomed Sunday beer, put down the heavy glass mug with a bang that nearly shattered it.

"Do you mean to tell me that you—even you—have been putting us through this ridiculous circus for the fun of it, when your mind was already made up?" he demanded furiously.

"Don't shout, dear boy—it will disturb Minnie in the kitchen. I wanted your views, naturally. I, of course, acted at once on impulse. I could not refuse the refuge of my heart and my home which are open to all, could I?" Astrea beamed tranquilly on them both, and Marc got to his feet with a barely stifled imprecation.

"You'll have to excuse me, aunt—I haven't the stomach for any more lunch, with or without custard. I'll pack my things and go back to London this afternoon, if you don't mind. I've had about as much as I can take of your histrionics, coupled with those confounded stars," he said, and walked out of the room.

"Custard?" murmured Astrea, looking quite bewildered.

"You're eating custard with your lamb instead of mint sauce," Charity said. She felt exhausted and also a little hysterical; there had been something faintly comic in Astrea's outrageous behaviour and her nephew's subsequent loss of temper.

"Marc is seldom rude to me," Astrea complained, sounding a little ill-used. "Would you think he still cares for Roma after all this time?"

"I don't know," Charity replied, the desire for laughter leaving her, "but if he does, you've scarcely helped to make things any easier, have you?"

"Now, don't *you* start, dear child," said Astrea fretfully. "Marc can stand a little hectoring—he hands it out himself when it suits him."

"I don't like unkindness," Charity said. "Marc's been very patient with you."

"O-ho!" exclaimed Astrea, delighted to have got a rise. "You have a little fondness for him, after all? This should be interesting when Roma comes home—not that you can hold a candle to her, my poor child."

Charity fought back her desire to follow Marc's example and lose her temper. Astrea was impossible in her present mood, but Charity knew there was nothing she would like better than to draw blood and complete the rout.

"I don't expect to compete with Mrs. Nixon in looks, or in any other way," she said quietly. "Shall I ring for Minnie to clear?"

"If you please," said Astrea graciously, resorting, as usual, to dignity when she knew she had gone too far. "You know, dear child, my stars for today forecast strife and opposition, and misunderstanding. I should have been warned, should I not?"

"Yes, you should."

Astrea knew when she was beaten. When the child looked

at her like that with grave, accusing eyes, and a polite
refusal to be blandished, it was better to leave well alone.
In any case she had had her amusement for the day, and
perhaps it had not been very entertaining, after all.

"I will go and make my peace with Marc," she announced
virtuously. "I shall persuade him, of course, to stay until
tomorrow."

Whether or not she had made her peace with her
nephew, Charity was not to know, but she did not succeed
in persuading him to stay. Charity, from the window,
watched him drive away half an hour later. He had not
stopped to say goodbye.

In the days that followed, Astrea seemed petulant and
uncertain. Having made her gesture, she was inclined to
regret it. She must, she said, offer hospitality, since it was
demanded of her, but there it would end. When Charity
suggested that she should move out of the room that had
once been Roma's, she was told not to be foolish.

"Roma is merely a visitor," Astrea said sweepingly.
"You, my dear child, are my spiritual daughter. Do not
forget it."

But for all this, Charity sensed her excited anticipation.
She might resist the implication that the return of the prodigal could in any way affect her, after all this time, but she
argued endlessly with Minnie on Roma's favorite dishes,
Roma's preference in wines, and her objection, when she
was last at Cleat, to Astrea's refusal to have a radio in the
house.

"Perhaps we should get a set," Astrea said grudgingly.
"My magnificent recordings should satisfy anyone, but the
young like this jazz, or jive, or whatever it's called."

A set was installed, not in the music-room, which would
have been sacrilege, but in the little study which Roma apparently used to use as her sitting-room.

"But if she's only coming on a visit—" Charity protested, her economical soul a little shocked, but Astrea
took up one of her grandiose attitudes.

"No matter!" she said. "The thing will come in handy afterwards. Me, I have no concern with things that happen in the world today, but you and Minnie might care to hear the news."

"She's really looking forward to Mrs. Nixon's return, isn't she?" Charity asked Minnie, as she helped to turn out the room that would be Roma's during her visit.

The old dresser's mouth pursed in discouraging lines.

"She likes the novelty of anything unexpected," she replied. "Miss Roma always made a lot of work. She'll make it again, I don't doubt."

"Well, I'll always give you a hand, Minnie," Charity said shyly. She was still uncertain as to whether the old woman had accepted her or not.

"H'm . . . maybe it'll come to that," Minnie said, without enthusiasm. "You'll find your nose out of joint, I shouldn't wonder, young miss."

"Not at all," Charity replied pleasantly. "I'm here as a paid companion, as you yourself have often pointed out. There's been no need for you to wait on me."

Minnie sniffed.

"I take my orders from Madam," she said. "If she fancied you as one of them spiritual how-d'you-do's she's always talking about, it weren't nothing to do with me. Had these fads all her life, has m'lady."

"She's lonely," Charity said gently, and the old woman left her polishing and dusting for a moment to give Charity a shrewd look.

"You're the only one that's understood her, I'll say that for you," she said gruffly. "Them others—took what they could get, and laughed behind her back, I shouldn't wonder. She wasn't always a figure of fun, wasn't m'lady."

"You're very devoted to her, aren't you?" Charity said.

Minnie shrugged.

"We've been through good times and bad together. That makes a bond," she said. "She romances a lot now, but she made a stir in her day, when all's said and done, not but what she doesn't get mixed in her dates. But it's sad, young miss, when the world forgets you. There's loneliness and heartbreak too, in clinging to the past. Miss Roma never understood that.''

''She was too young, perhaps.''

''No younger than what you are, but Madam spoilt her. All this talk of the money and then making conditions— but Mr. Marc was never one to fall in with her whims, and so they both found out.''

''Mrs. Nixon could have married Mr. Marc on his own terms,'' Charity said tentatively, and Minnie sniffed again.

''When you've had a fortune dangled in front of your nose, you, maybe, don't think so clear,'' she answered. ''You be warned, young miss. Her money is m'lady's only weapon now. I wouldn't like to see you come unstuck, like the others.''

It was the first intimation Minnie had ever given that she considered Charity any different from her predecessors, and the girl's heart warmed to her.

''I'm not concerned with the money, Minnie,'' she said shyly. ''I know Mrs. Stubbs is given to—fancies.''

''And don't you let her hear you calling her that!'' the old woman snapped, reverting to her usual manner, but her eyes rested for a moment with grudging tolerance upon Charity, before she resumed her task of cleaning.

MARC WAS not coming down again until the courts rose just before Easter, and the day before Good Friday Roma Nixon arrived at Cleat, unheralded, having driven from the docks in a hired car with a pile of luggage.

Charity was arranging flowers in the music-room when she heard the sudden commotion and saw Astrea sweep into the hall and clasp someone to her bosom in the all-too-familiar embrace. There were exclamations, cries of protest and delight, then they came into the music-room together.

"Roma, my dear, dear child! Let me look at you!"
Astrea cried, oblivious, as usual, of the presence of a third
person, and Charity, forgotten, let her eyes dwell curiously
on the newcomer and they widened as they gazed.

Roma was tall and exquisite from her flaming head of
hair to her expensively shod feet; her face had the lovely
purity of a mediaeval painting, with its full lips and
smooth contours, and there was something oddly familiar
in the expression. It was not until later that Charity realized
that Astrea had once been like this, that she might in truth
have said to Roma, as she had to Charity: "You are my
lost youth. . . ."

"The same . . . the same . . ." Astrea was saying,
devouring the girl's face with moist eyes. "Oh, my darling,
such a long time! So much water under the bridge . . . so
many wasted years. . . ."

"You don't change, either, Astrea," Roma said with a
smile. "And I remember that old tea-gown seven years
ago." She spoke in a slow, rather husky voice, and her
years in the States had given her a slight accent which was
rather attractive.

"Seven years!" Astrea said, and bestowed upon her
another violent embrace.

Roma extricated herself languidly and her eyes rested for
a moment on Charity.

"Who's that?" she asked.

"A little girl called Charity Child. She's my companion,"
Astrea said with careless indifference, and Roma's finely
pencilled eyebrows rose.

"That makes you sound very elderly, Astrea," she
remarked with amusement. "What do you need a companion for?"

"I was lonely," Astrea said with unusual simplicity, and
Charity, who had been half-way across the room to shake
hands, went back to her flowers.

"Did you miss me?" Roma asked idly, her eyes wander-
ing round the familiar room, marking each remembered

item, the professional photographs, the framed programs and yellowing manuscripts, the plaster plaques of musicians' heads in relief on the walls.

Charity watched her surreptitiously. The mink, the jewels, the inviting whiff of some provocative scent as she moved, put her in another world, the world of pampered women who had never been obliged to work for a living. Just for a moment Charity knew an unfamiliar pang of envy.

"Not at all!" Astrea retorted, remembering that she had nursed a grievance for seven years. "You treated me abominably! You were my daughter in all but fact, and I would have made you my heiress."

"But you didn't, Astrea. You offered me a bone, then snatched it away."

"Because Marc wouldn't have you on those terms and you didn't care enough to take him on his."

"Oh, yes, Marc . . . is he married?" Roma asked softly, sinking into a chair by the fire, where she sat, smoking one cigarette after another. She appeared to have Astrea's gift for discussing her private affairs before a stranger.

"No, he is not, and he will be here for Easter."

Roma's long lashes veiled her eyes for a moment. She had heavy lids, Charity noticed, smooth and full and very white.

"Does he know I'll be here?" she asked.

"Naturally," Astrea replied. "He has quite got over you, my dear, in fact he—" Her eyes slid to Charity, and Roma's followed.

"In fact he what?" she prompted, looking suddenly alert, but Astrea only smiled as if she had scored a point.

"Never mind," she said, and for some reason Roma seemed suddenly to annoy her.

"This dear child," she went on, gesturing towards Charity, "is my spiritual daughter, just as you once were. She is very *simpatica*. I'm thinking of adopting her."

For the first time Roma Nixon gave Charity her full attention. Her eyes travelled deliberately over the girl, appraising, discarding. She had in that moment, Charity thought uncomfortably, Marc's own gift for applying silent judgment.

"Really?" she said with her slight, husky drawl. "And are you thinking of leaving her your money, too?"

"Why not?" Astrea retorted. "You have no need of it now, with all those dollars."

Roma's gaze focused gently and a little wearily on the old painted face.

"There aren't any dollars, Astrea," she said.

There was a pause while Astrea irritably jangled her many charms.

"What do you mean, there aren't any dollars?" she demanded then. "That old husband of yours was rolling in money—it's the only reason you married him."

Charity went on arranging her flowers, feeling acutely embarrassed, but they had already forgotten her. Roma lay back in her chair and smiled.

"He changed his will before he died," she said. "I seem unlucky over the question of wills, don't I, honey?"

"You mean he left you nothing?"

"Not a cent, beyond the marriage settlement which he couldn't touch. When that's gone—" She spread out her hands expressively, broad, rather ugly hands with predatory fingers, the only blemish in what was near perfection.

"Who gets the money, then?"

"His children and his first wife's family. They never liked me. They paid my passage back to England to get rid of me, and that was all, so you see, dear Astrea, I had to fling myself upon your mercy."

"*Monstrous!*" Astrea cried, her mood completely changing again, and she flung out both her hands in one of her favorite gestures of beneficence. "My poor, poor child! How cruel, how *scandalous*! But you shall make your home here, as you used to . . . you will be my spiritual daughter again . . . my lost youth. . . ."

"Two spiritual daughters?" said Roma with amusement.

"Why not, why not?" exclaimed Astrea, clapping her hands. "The stars foretell it, for you are Gemini—Gemini, the twins. You shall be sister to my dear Ganymede, and she to you."

Roma's swift glance in Charity's direction said plainly that she thought such a conceit preposterous, but she smiled indulgently on Astrea.

"Do you still rule your life by the stars?" she asked lazily. "You haven't changed one little bit. May I go to my room and unpack? I suppose it's the usual one."

"No, dear child, Charity has that," Astrea replied, adding as a reminder that her hasty offer of a home was not to be imposed upon. "You must share and share alike. Charity has first call upon me, now."

"I doubt, all the same, if she would care to share my old bedroom, so I'll settle for the room you've chosen for me," said Roma indifferently, but the glance she gave Charity as she got to her feet was very shrewd and not indifferent at all.

They met again in the music-room alone, before Astrea joined them for dinner. Roma had changed into something svelte and elegant. She looked expensive and entirely at her ease. Charity, on the other hand, wearing one of the charming but undistinguished frocks Astrea had bought her, felt awkward and immature.

"Well, my spiritual twin, or whatever the quaint relationship is supposed to be, we'd best get acquainted," Roma said, and lighted a cigarette. Her hands were well kept, but the faint nicotine stains on her fingers gave evidence that she was a chain-smoker.

"I'm sure you know Astrea well enough not to take these fancies seriously," Charity replied. "I—I'd like you to know from the start, Mrs. Nixon, that I perfectly well realize that I haven't supplanted you."

"Very civil of you, but prim and self-effacing like the well-trained companion. *Are* you a companion, by the way?"

"Yes, your aunt employs me—oh, I'm sorry, I was getting you confused with Marc."

"Marc?" Roma's eyes narrowed slightly. "Do you call him by his given name, too?"

"It was Astrea's wish."

"I see. And is it Astrea's wish that you should also— supplant me—in her nephew's affections?"

Charity colored slightly.

"Of course not! We disliked one another intensely to start with, as a matter of fact."

"Yes, he can be pretty riling upon occasion, can't he? A very biting tongue, has Mr. Marc Gentle."

Charity said nothing. She did not want to be drawn into a discussion of this kind with the girl Marc had once wanted to marry, nor did she care for the implication which seemed to lie behind Roma's perfectly pleasant manner.

"How did you meet Astrea?" Roma said, changing the subject. Charity gave her a brief, rather halting account of Astrea's visit to the shop in the Charing Cross Road and its subsequent results, and saw those delicate eyebrows lift in sceptical amusement.

"How very opportune for you," she drawled.

"You don't believe me?"

"Oh, I believe you, honey, it sounds just the sort of crazy thing Astrea would do. You must have your wits about you more than your looks would imply."

"I needed a job," said Charity bleakly. "When you have your living to earn, Mrs. Nixon, you aren't so particular as to the way in which a job is offered."

"I'm sure," said Roma with amusement. "And since

you seem to be on familiar terms with everyone who visits here, you'd best start calling me Roma. Now, what's all this about the money?''

"The money?"

"Oh, don't be dumb! Has Astrea changed her will?"

"I haven't the least idea."

"No? And what has our learned friend to say about this latest foible?"

"You'd better ask him yourself when he comes down," said Charity coldly, and Roma laughed and lit another cigarette, offering her case as an afterthought to Charity, who shook her head.

"No vices?" Roma mocked. "You're a bit of an oddity, I fancy, Charity Child. Incidentally, didn't you get teased to death at school about that name? How have you gotten it?"

"Perhaps my mother had a warped sense of humor," retorted Charity coolly, and Roma laughed again.

"Not so dumb after all, are you, honey?" she said. "We should get along."

Charity doubted it. Roma Nixon would be pleasant for as long as it suited her, she thought, but she was already making it clear what she considered Charity's position in the house should be.

When Astrea joined them, Charity was told to dispense the sherry, but Roma refused.

"A highball for me, please," she said. "I never could stand this stuff; it gives me a liver."

"Highball?" repeated Astrea vaguely.

"Scotch. Haven't you any in the house darling?"

Charity was sent to fetch a bottle of whisky and they sat for longer than usual over their drinks while Minnie impatiently sounded the gong, then poked her face round the door to say the dinner was spoiling.

"Good old Minnie, she doesn't change, either—do you still have those back-chat arguments?" Roma said as they sat down to dinner.

"One changes less as one gets older, I suppose," said Astrea, sighing a little. "And you, my dear, dear child—do you think you have changed?"

"Oh, yes," Roma answered with amusement. "I've changed. Seven years in the States with the Nixon fortune at your back does a lot for a girl, you know. And Marc—has he not changed, either?"

Astrea frowned into her plate. She was not sure Charity thought, how she wanted to answer that.

"Naturally he has altered," she said then. "I daresay you will find him more to your taste. He's made a considerable success at the Bar, you know, and is taking silk. He makes a great deal of money these days."

"Does he, now?" said Roma softly. "And still unmarried . . . should I take that as a compliment, honey?"

"I wish," said Astrea irritably, "you would not address me as that—so undignified—so reminiscent of those dreadful American films—and you will take it as a compliment, I don't doubt, whether it is or it isn't."

"We'll see," Roma said, unperturbed. "You'll have to get used to my Americanisms, I'm afraid, Astrea. One picks up the idiom so quickly. Charity tells me she dislikes poor Marc."

"I said, if you remember, that we both disliked each other to start with," Charity corrected her, aware of Astrea's sudden interest.

"I was forgetting the distinction," said Roma with an amused smile. "So now you find you don't dislike our learned friend so much? And have his feelings suffered a sea change, too?"

Charity was saved from having to reply by Astrea taking it upon herself to settle all their affairs with one of her misleading statements.

"Marc is quite taken with my little Ganymede," she said, blowing Charity a kiss across the table. "He comes quite regularly for weekends now. Last time he brought her a present."

"Really?" Roma drawled, giving the girl a speculative glance.

"It was a second-hand book of verse," Charity said hastily, judging by the glint in Astrea's eye that she was quite prepared to embroider further.

"Oh, I see," Roma replied, with a twist to her full lips. "Marc always did have this dreary taste for poetry. So you play up to him, honey? Well, it's one way of getting a man, I suppose."

"I happen to like poetry," Charity said stiffly, and Astrea shook an arch finger at them both.

"Never bicker over a man, my dear, dear children—so *bourgeois*," she said. "Aquarius and Gemini do not make for Harmonious Grouping, but you must rise above it. Do you not think, my dear Roma, that Charity has a face like a sad pierrot?"

"Not particularly," Roma said shortly. "Is that what Marc says?"

"No, no, it was my own discovery, but he recognized her by that at the station. I'm surprised you don't catch the resemblance, dear child. You used to be so quick to follow my word-pictures."

"Maybe I've lost the art," said Roma, beginning to look bored. "Let's talk of something else, dear Astrea— Ganymede, or whatever outlandish name you call her, is looking embarrassed."

The talk became general, so far as any conversation which included Astrea could be said to be that. Roma spoke of her life in America and the vast difference in living conditions she had found there. She could talk well, when she chose; her descriptions were economical but vivid, and she brought a pleasing caustic wit to her anecdotes about the people she had met; a wit which, Charity thought, would match Marc's. She had not, it seemed, thought very highly of the States, despite the comfort and luxury that money had brought. She had been homesick for Cleat, she said, and even the stolidity of English country life.

"Funny, isn't it?" she finished, with a wry little smile. "When I was twenty or so, I thought money bought everything. America seemed like a dream too good to be true."

"And you found, my child, that money cannot buy happiness," said Astrea, her eyes moist in the candlelight.

"Don't kid yourself, honey, money can buy happiness all right—lots of it," Roma retorted. "It's when you're suddenly left with none that the rub comes."

"If you'd stayed in America you could have married more dollars," said Astrea, suddenly peevish. "With your looks it should not have been hard to find another rich tycoon."

"Perhaps," drawled Roma, with a little sidelong glance at Charity, "I would prefer to marry an Englishmàn, this time."

Charity excused herself early that evening, feeling that there must be many things the other two would want to discuss in private, but upstairs in the delightful room which had once been Roma's, she sat for a long time before undressing, brooding uneasily upon the future, disturbed, she found surprisingly, more on Marc's account than her own. She could not care greatly, she told herself reasonably, what became of a man she had, until lately, disliked so much; all the same, she did not want him to be hurt all over again.

When she was in bed she reached for the anthology of verse he had given her and carefully read the poems he had picked out for her on his last visit.

ROMA, AS well as Astrea, breakfasted in bed the next morning, and Charity got up early to give Minnie a hand with the household chores, for, since it was Good Friday, the daily women expected time off. Minnie had always in-

'sisted on her rights in the matter of Astrea's breakfast tray, so Charity took up Roma's.

The room seemed filled with cabin trunks and open suitcases, and Roma herself, propped against her pillows with yesterday's morning paper, waved a helpless hand towards the heap of luggage.

"How shall I manage?" she demanded in mock despair. "I've been used to a maid all these years—I'm quite out of the way of doing things for myself."

"I'll help you unpack and get sorted out, if you like," Charity offered willingly.

"Would you really? That would be kind of you. Can you launder and press efficiently, by any chance?"

Charity wondered if this was another hint as to the difference of their respective positions in the house, but she answered pleasantly:

"I see to my own clothes, naturally. I'll be glad to press anything you may need immediately, but you won't unpack everything, will you?"

"Why ever not? My clothes must look like rags as it is, and there's another cabin trunk coming. The hired automobile couldn't take it all."

Charity glanced with slight dismay at the hanging accommodation of Astrea's spare room. The cupboards were adequate but not designed for an extensive wardrobe.

"I only thought that if you are just on a visit, there must be a good deal of stuff you wouldn't need," she said, and Roma ran an idle hand through the burnished waves of her magnificent hair.

"What makes you think I'm just on a visit?" she asked with a yawn. "Didn't you hear me tell Astrea I had nowhere else to go? This used to be my home, you know."

"Yes, of course," said Charity, flushing. "Well, I expect Noakes can move another wardrobe in from one of the disused rooms."

"I shouldn't bother," Roma said. "In a little while we'll change over, don't you think? Astrea furnished your room for me, you know."

"I did offer—" began Charity uncomfortably, but Roma broke in with a dazzling smile:

"Of course you did, but we couldn't upset poor Astrea my very first evening, could we? Things will adjust themselves, you'll see."

"Yes, of course."

Charity stood a little uncertainly, wondering whether to go or not. There was something odd about the other girl's face this morning, and she realized with a small sense of shock that, like many red-haired people, Roma had colorless brows and lashes. Without the beautifully applied pencil and mascara, her face looked strangely naked.

"You needn't wait," she said, returning to her paper, leaving her breakfast to get cold. It was quite pleasantly spoken but Charity left the room feeling rather like a dismissed lady's maid.

She spoke to Minnie about the problem of the luggage, but the old woman merely grunted.

"It can bide where it is," she said. "You can hang clothes on them cabin trunks, can't you? No call to turn the house upside down for a visit."

"I think she means to stay," Charity said, and Minnie grunted again.

"That'll be for Madam to decide," she sniffed, "and if she's any sense she won't start all *that* nonsense over again."

"But things aren't as we supposed," Charity said, feeling that, unwelcome though she might be, Roma needed some support. "There aren't any dollars, after all."

"So I believe—so now she's after m'lady's little bit, and Mr. Marc's too, I shouldn't wonder. Them Yankee in-laws got browned-off, and the old man, too."

"Oh, Minnie, that's not very kind. I thought you used to like Mrs. Nixon."

"I know her better than you do, young miss. Liking is one thing, trust is another. Miss Roma wouldn't have made many bones as to what she was after, and they saw through her," Minnie said, and stumped off to the kitchen to attend to her own chores.

Charity spent the early part of the afternoon helping Roma unpack, marvelling at so much lavishness.

"You look sad," Roma said a little mockingly. "Does all this make you envious?"

"No," Charity answered simply. "I was sorry on your account. It was very wrong of your husband, I should have said, to—to give with one hand and take away with the other."

"Would you, Charity? But life is like that, haven't you found—or are you still too young?"

"No, but I don't think I've ever wanted the same things as you."

"That's just as well," Roma observed with a certain dryness. "For then we won't tread on each other's toes."

"What do you mean?"

"Only that I mean to get what I want, and if it happens to be what you are after as well, it will be just too bad."

"If you're thinking of Astrea's money—" Charity began with the candid baldness of an adolescent, and Roma smiled and patted her cheek.

"I wasn't thinking of Astrea's money," she said with that attractive, husky drawl. "There might be other concerns of mine to keep your hands off, too, honey. Now, be a dear and give some of these things a press for me, or I won't have a decent thing to wear when Marc comes."

He was to arrive on Saturday, Charity knew. She had looked forward to the Easter Vacation, the walks on the downs, the poetry readings, the renewal of a companionship which she was already beginning to confuse with that of her father, but now she was doubtful. It had, of course, been quite unnecessary and rather ridiculous for Roma to have issued veiled warnings where Marc was concerned, but she was not going to enjoy the role of gooseberry which was bound to be forced on her from time to time.

She kept out of the way for most of that afternoon, not wishing to be a witness of that first meeting between them, but even so he surprised them all together just before dinner. Astrea had been playing one of her records, so that they did not hear the car, and he walked in upon them unannounced.

"Hullo, Charity Child," he said, having acknowledged his aunt's preoccupied greeting, for she was busy searching for a mislaid recording, then he turned suddenly and saw Roma.

She had risen from her chair by the fire and taken a step forward, hands outstretched to him, and then stood, waiting. It had been a dull day and the light was already beginning to fade. In the mixture of dusk and firelight her lifted face was curiously arresting, and Charity, who watched with a sensation of trespass, could have sworn there were tears in her eyes.

"Marc . . ." she said softly.

He stood rigidly where he was, and the skin seemed to tighten over his angular features. Charity saw his nervous, bony hands clench for a moment at his sides before he put them in his pockets.

"Hullo, Roma—so you've arrived," he said casually.

She crossed the room to meet him and her hands rested lightly on his shoulders.

"Marc . . . dear Marc . . ." she said, and lifted her face like a child.

When he did not move she asked, with a little broken laugh:

"Aren't you going to kiss me—for old time's sake—or are you still cross with me after seven years?"

He bent his head then and kissed her lightly on the forehead.

"I was never cross with you, Roma," he replied coolly. "It's a word associated with spoilt children, and you were never that."

"You used to say I was spoilt."

"So you were, abominably, but you were never a child. Well, let's look at you. H'm . . . the gods are still kind. You were a beautiful girl—you are now a very beautiful woman." He spoke with calm deliberation, as though he was merely concerned with the assessment of an admired work of art, but he still kept his hands hidden in his pockets, and there was a little nervous twitch at the corner of his mouth.

Charity turned away and began to help Astrea look for the missing record, astonished at the shock to her own feelings. Not so long ago she would have welcomed the knowledge that disagreeable Marc Gentle was capable of being hurt, but now she found she could not bear to watch him. Was he still in love with Roma, she wondered, with unexpected pain, or had the sight of her beauty simply reminded him of old desires? Busy with her own thoughts, she moved a pile of records carelessly, and one fell to the floor, snapping in two.

"Really, dear child, how unutterably careless!" Astrea exclaimed, swooping on the broken record. "I thought I could trust you with these precious things. What can you have been thinking of?"

"I'm so sorry—so terribly sorry," stammered Charity, nearly in tears. "I will replace it, of course."

"You cannot replace it—it is one of the old Boncelli recordings, out of circulation long ago," said Astrea, her face wearing the expression of a sorrowing tragedienne. "All your generation are ignoramuses—*vandals*! You care nothing for the genius of Boncelli, any more than you care for the genius of Astrea—jazz, jive, scuffle—those are your standards!"

"I think you mean skiffle, aunt," Marc said with a cer-

tain amusement, and he took the broken pieces from
Astrea's hands and tossed them into the wastepaper
basket. "Pack up the dramatics, Astrea, the child didn't
break the thing on purpose."

Astrea was silent from sheer surprise at the gravity in his
voice, and watched with interested curiosity as her nephew
gently brush a finger along Charity's wet lashes.

"Don't be upset," he said with a sardonic little smile.
"There are worse things than broken records—broken
hearts, for instance."

Roma was still standing where he had left her, smoke
curling upwards from the cigarette she had just lighted.
She, like Astrea, was watching, but the suddenly tense expression on her face was not one of curiosity.

"Was that intended as a warning?" she asked with a
lightness that did not quite come off.

"I don't think so," Marc replied casually. "It was more
in the nature of a statement. Cheer up, Charity Child, my
aunt won't eat you up! It might have been far more serious
had you smashed an Astrea recording. Let me give you a
glass of sherry."

"I don't—" began Charity, uncertainly.

"You don't drink, of course! Never mind, this shall be
regarded as medicinal."

She took the wine he poured out for her because a refusal would only have added to the fuss. Whether he was
paying her this attention to mask his own feelings, or merely
to annoy Roma, she could not decide, but she wanted to
escape as hurriedly as possible from the limelight that
should have been the other girl's. She took her sherry and
sat down quietly in a corner of the room.

"Well!" Marc said. "We should all drink to the return
of the prodigal, I suppose. What's your tipple these days,
Roma?"

"But we must have champagne!" cried Astrea, clapping
her hands. "Run and ask Minnie for the glasses, Charity

dear, and tell her to keep back dinner. What an occasion!
What joy for Eastertide! Hurry, dear child—tell Minnie to
pick the right vintage."

"I think," her nephew said with a quizzical lift of one
eyebrow, "I had better do the selecting myself," and he
followed Charity out of the room.

Roma sat down with idle grace and, throwing her
cigarette into the fire, lighted another.

"Is he giving your little companion a whirl?" she enquired lazily.

Astrea jingled her charms.

"A whirl? I do not understand your American jargon,
dear child. What do you think of Marc, after all this
time?"

Roma shrugged.

"What should I think, dear Astrea? He wasn't exactly
enthusiastic with his welcome. Has this girl lost her silly
little heart to him?"

"Now that," said Astrea, with easy invitation, "is
something you could very well find out for me. They were
not *simpatica* at the beginning, but emotions can change,
can they not?"

"Are you at your little schemes again, honey? I'll have
to warn you that I'll spike them."

"I don't know what you mean, dear child, and I wish
you would not call me 'honey'. Have you no faith in
yourself, Roma? Do you not know that you and someone
like that little girl of mine are poles apart?"

"I would imagine so," said Roma with amusement.
"But the question is—which pole will Marc prefer?"

"Does it matter?" Astrea asked, dismissing the question
with her customary vagueness.

"Yes, I think it does," Roma said, lighting another
cigarette.

Outside in the hall, Marc had stopped Charity on her
way to the kitchen.

"Why are you upset?" he asked. "Because you broke one of my aunt's records?"

"Well, naturally! I know those old recordings can't be replaced."

"I don't think that was the only reason. Roma's return worries you, doesn't it?"

She was too honest or, perhaps, too inexperienced to evade that question.

"It's not my place to be concerned with Astrea's visitors," she replied a little primly. "But I don't think Mrs. Nixon likes me."

His face, in the dim light of the hall, had its old look of mockery.

"How correct you are, Charity Child," he said. "But you should grow out of this idea that strangers don't take to you. Look at me!"

She took him literally and looked, her wide eyes grave and a little troubled, and he suddenly ran a careless hand over her smooth dark head.

"Absurd child, aren't you?" he said.

"I'm not a child," she told him gravely, and he gave a little impatient sigh.

"No, I suppose not," he said. "Well, we'd better see about that champagne. Does Easter mean something to you, Charity?"

"Oh, yes," she replied, her face lighting up. "My father always said it meant more than Christmas—Resurrection, hope, the beginning of new life."

He gave her a curious look.

"Yes . . . well . . ." he said, and his mouth had softened into a half-bitter expression of tenderness. "I doubt if the rest of the household feels quite that way. Run along and fetch those glasses. Minnie won't be best pleased at her dinner being kept waiting."

CHAPTER FIVE

EASTER MORNING broke fresh and sparkling, the very epitome of the spring of the year. Charity had filled the house with catkin and pussy willow and great bowls of daffodils which had just blossomed in the garden. She slipped quietly out of the house to church before Astrea or Roma were awake and, to her surprise, Marc accompanied her.

They walked through the fields in the early morning sunshine, and the bells from the village church pealed a greeting to the day.

"I didn't think you'd want to go to church," Charity said.

"Didn't you, Charity? Perhaps your father's definition of Easter inspired me. Do you remember Housman?

> *'In summer time on Bredon*
> *The bells they sound so clear . . .'* "

"But that was so sad," she said. "They wouldn't listen until his love rose up so early and went to church alone."

> " *'They tolled the one bell only,*
> *Groom there was none to see . . .'*

For heaven's sake, we're getting morbid, and Housman is outdated now, so I'm told. Did you know, Charity, that it's supposed to be a sinister sign when two people start quoting verse to one another?"

"No," she replied innocently, pausing to pick colts'-foot

from the bank. "People, I've found, don't care much for peotry any more. Does Roma?"

"Roma?" He frowned, obviously disliking the introduction of personalities. "Roma never had a taste for verse," he said, with a certain hardness. "I just try myself out on you, my dear. Didn't you know that all poetry lovers like to quote to an admiring audience? It's a form of conceit."

"Is it?" said Charity, swinging her long legs over a stile with ingenuous disregard for the briefness of her skirt.

"Perhaps—perhaps not," he answered ambiguously. "What long legs you have, grandmother!"

"All the better to race you with, my dear!" she retorted promptly, and started to run, but he soon caught up with her.

"This is not the proper spirit in which to attend a service," he rebuked her severely, but she laughed and was happy again. She must, she thought, remember not to mention Roma unless he did himself.

At the little lych-gate which led to the church he took the colt's-foot from her and placed it in his button-hole.

"It doesn't look at all right," she protested doubtfully, but he only grinned and shepherded her firmly into the church.

When the service was over they stayed to speak to the Rector, who lamented the absence of Madame Astrea. In Cleat, at least, Astrea was not forgotten. She seldom interested herself in the village affairs, but for all that she was their one prized celebrity.

"What a pity she won't go out more," Charity said with genuine regret as they walked through the sunny churchyard. "She could enjoy her fame in the village."

"When you've enjoyed fame in the capitals of Europe the small puddle of a Sussex village is hardly sufficient," observed Marc dryly.

"No, I suppose not."

They walked home the way they had come, through

grass still soaked with dew, and up the steep incline of Cleat Hill. They reached the crest of the hill to see a cherry tree in full flower sketched in delicate beauty against the sky.

"And this, of course, I can't resist," said Marc as they stopped to admire, and he began to quote:

> " 'Loveliest of trees, the cherry now
> Is hung with bloom along the bough,
> And stands about the woodland ride
> Wearing white for Eastertide. . . .'

What a genuine countryman Housman was!"

"You have a special fondness for him, I think," Charity said. "And yet I would never really associate you with country things."

"Wouldn't you, Charity Child? But I wasn't always a street sparrow like you. When my mother was alive we lived in country much like this. We even had our own cherry tree in the garden."

"Did you?" She glanced at him quickly, seeing the fleeting nostalgia in his face, and remembered that he had loved and missed his mother.

"Was your childhood spent in the country?" she asked gently.

"Yes," he said, and she sighed.

"How I envy you. My father was a countryman, too, but our life was spent in towns, trying to scrape a living from his music—teaching the piano, playing in café orchestras—anything that gave him time to compose the stuff he never could sell."

He glanced at her profile as she swung along beside him, seeing again the melancholy look of Pierrot, the plaintive brows, the air of lost forlornness.

"Don't regret it," he told her with gentleness. "Your

father must have given you all you would have found for yourself, and more, for I think he gave you appreciation—and values."

"Values?"

"Yes. For a young girl just turned twenty, you have, I should imagine, remarkable values."

It was a strange conversation and, for Charity, was accompanied by the odd sensation that he was no stranger, that walking to church and back on Easter Day had forged a slender bond between them.

But once back at Cleat House the illusion vanished. Astrea and Roma were both breakfasting downstairs in varying stages of undress, and Roma twitted Marc with charming impudence for going to church. The atmosphere became, all at once, slightly artificial, and Charity, although she tried to share Astrea's exaggerated delight in the colored eggs which Minnie had dyed for them, felt foolish and insincere.

"Such a glorious day!" Roma exclaimed, stretching her bare, firmly rounded arms above her head. "Will you take me to the sea, Marc?"

"Not over the holiday," he retorted, slicing the top off a scarlet egg with a deft twist of the wrist. "All main roads to Brighton will be hell on earth with the Easter coastal traffic."

"What can we do, then?" she said plaintively. "I seem to remember of old the deadly inertia of a British Sunday."

"You're used to the exhausting hustle of the States, my dear. In England we still like to think the sabbath a day of rest," Marc replied with a grin. However he had reacted last night to Roma's arrival, he seemed to have himself well in hand now, Charity thought, taking a guilty pleasure in the fact that Roma's careful toilet seemed to be making little impression.

"You will, dear child, have to accustom yourself again to the quiet of Cleat if you want to stay," Astrea chimed in with unexpected asperity, and Marc smiled.

"I daresay Roma has other, more exciting plans," he observed. "When she's paid you her little courtesy visit, Astrea, she'll be off to the bright lights and the pursuits of the idle rich."

"But she is no longer a rich woman, dear boy," said Astrea, remembering, with satisfaction, that her nephew had not yet learnt that piece of news.

His eyebrows went up.

"The dollars not so numerous as was at first supposed?" he said with a touch of irony.

"The dollars were very numerous," said Roma, with her husky drawl. "Wilbur saw fit to leave me nothing, that's all."

Marc pushed back his plate and wiped his mouth with deliberation.

"I see," he said then, and his eyes, resting on Roma with an attention that was now undivided, were shrewd and alert and rather hard. "Didn't you have lawyers to advise you?"

She shrugged her shapely shoulders and her smile was a little bitter.

"Your legal mind reacting first, as always," she said. "No, I didn't have lawyers. It didn't occur to me that my husband would change his will. When he was dead it was too late. Oh, I got me an attorney then, double quick, but he couldn't do anything. Wilbur had tied everything, nice and tight, and his folks had never liked me."

"How American you've become," said Marc absently, then he leaned forward, quizzing her as if she was in the witness-box.

"Does that mean that you have nothing—that you're in precisely the same position as you were seven years ago?" he asked.

There was a hint of humility, or was it invitation, in her eyes before she lowered her heavy lids and answered softly:

"Yes, Marc."

"I see," he said again.

"Does it make a difference?"

"To me? Perhaps—perhaps not."

The sound Charity's spoon made as she drove it though her empty egg-shell seemed like a pistol shot in the small silence. "Really, dear child!" exclaimed Astrea, annoyed by the interruption of such a promising little drama. "*Must* you behave so uncouthly?"

"It's an old superstition. It—it lets the witches out," Charity excused herself, knowing how irrelevant and absurd the remark must sound. Only Marc threw her an involuntary smile; Roma frowned impatiently, and Astrea said with pardonable irritation:

"Witches in *eggs*! What on earth are you talking about?"

Charity tactfully refrained from making any answer, and Roma held out her hand to Marc across the table, turning it palm upward in a small gesture of supplication.

"You'd like to say I got my deserts, wouldn't you, Marc?" she said softly. "I treated you badly—and Astrea, too. Now I'm paid back in my own coin."

For a moment his expression softened, and Charity saw how he must once have looked at her, with understanding and a half-rueful tenderness.

"I wouldn't kick anyone who was down," he told her gently. "But you won't stay down, Roma. You still have most of the weapons in your locker, even if you didn't fool your astute American husband. Well, what are you going to do for cash?"

"She will stay here, of course," boomed Astrea, who had been left long enough out of the conversation. "Cleat was home to Roma once, and can be again. You shall even have your old allowance back, dear child—that marriage settlement must be invested—Marc shall see to it for you."

"I'm not a broker, Astrea," he said mildly, then turned back to Roma. "So there is something?"

"Nothing that brings in much more than a pittance," Roma replied negligently. "It's already invested in American stock. I suppose I can get it transferred over here?"

"That will have to be gone into. Well, are you proposing to make Cleat your home again?"

"What else can I do?"

"You could work," he said unexpectedly, and her beautifully pencilled eyebrows rose in delicate twin arches.

"Doing what? Would you suggest I took a post of companion, like Charity here?"

"Charity, and girls like her, at least keep their self-respect," he retorted with sudden hardness, and a little muscle jerked under one of Roma's eyes.

"You haven't forgotten—or forgiven, have you?" she said with gentle regret.

"Your type of woman sometimes makes it difficult to do that," he replied quietly. "I'm not reproaching you, my dear. I only wondered whether, after all this time, life had taught you anything."

"Oh, yes," she said with a hardness that matched his. "Life has taught me a great deal; one great truth being that unless you go after what you want yourself, no one else will root for you."

"And do you know yet what you want?" he asked.

"Oh, yes," she said with a little smile. "I haven't changed."

Charity got up, trying to find an excuse to leave them. It was perpetually disturbing, she thought angrily, this habit they all had of ignoring her presence when they wanted to discuss their affairs. At least Marc might have the common decency to wait until she was out of the room.

"Sit down, child, and don't fidget," commanded

Astrea, who had no intention of allowing the discussion to be diverted again, but Charity refused to remain an unwilling listener any longer.

"Minnie will need help with the beds as the daily women don't come on Sundays," she said firmly, adding, as she reached the door: "In any case, I should have thought you would have preferred to—to discuss Mrs. Nixon's affairs alone."

She saw Marc looking at her with the old mockery. He was, already, quite a different person from the man who had quoted Housman under the cherry tree.

"Haven't you learnt that the perfect companion has no ears?" he asked with teasing kindness.

"Like a well-trained servant," Roma added with an exaggerated drawl, and as the door closed behind Charity, Marc said sharply:

"That was unforgivable!"

THEY WERE, Charity thought during the following week, an ill-assorted household. Marc and Roma were polite enough on the surface, but in Roma's case, at least, there seemed to be an undercurrent of resentment which might at any moment lead to an explosion, and Astrea, delighting in a situation which relieved her own boredom, cast hopeful red herrings across the conversation. Charity, trying hard to efface her own personality in the character of paid companion, found, however that she was drawn, despite herself, into the family arguments. Astrea's fulsome insistence on the girl's place in her affection was difficult to meet with equanimity under the quizzical regard of the other two, for each in their own way, Charity thought, viewed her with suspicion, and Roma at any rate looked complacent when Astrea, as sometimes happened, had a revulsion of feeling, and reminded her new spiritual daughter that she was there on sufferance.

Marc found her, after one of these rebuffs, sitting on the

steps of the ornate porch, gazing out to the line of the downs, and looking much as she had when he had first seen her on the station platform, in a graceful curve of melancholy, her long legs twisted under her.

"Not so easy, is it, Pierrot?" he said.

"Pierrot?" She raised her face and looked at him with those dark grey eyes clouded now with uncertainty.

"You take to yourself the traditional attitude when you are troubled," he said. "Do my aunt's vagaries worry you?"

"It's sometimes difficult to know where one stands," she admitted. "I think, perhaps, your aunt likes to use me as a whip for Roma."

His eyebrows lifted.

"Do you, now? That's very perspicacious of you. And do you mind being used as a whip?"

She flushed, hearing the mockery in his voice.

"I'd thought she was fond of me," she said, and he gave a small exclamation of impatience.

"Oh, my dear child," he said, "be your age! You did very well as a substitute, but you can hardly expect to compete with Spiritual Daughter Number One!"

"No," she said, and he experienced that old desire to shake her.

"Is it still material benefits, or have you a misguided affection for my aunt?" he asked, and saw her blink.

"You won't give me the benefit of the doubt, even now, will you?" she said.

His face, in the April sunshine, took on a brittle hardness as if it masked a softer, more tender impulse.

"What I think about you scarcely matters any more, my dear," he answered. "I would sooner you didn't get hurt, that's all."

"And you?" she said, responding at once to that suggestion of consideration. "Will you get hurt—again?"

But she did not know him well enough to trespass, she realized immediately. His concern for her had been kindly

impersonal, while hers for him had been born of closer
ties.

"My private life is scarcely any business of yours," he
answered coldly. "Concern yourself with the job for which
you are paid and you'll come to no harm."

He could, she thought unhappily, put her in her place
more firmly than ever his aunt might do. She did not need
to be reminded of her position in the household; she merely
found it difficult, at times, to know what it was.

"Do you think you're a match for Roma when it comes
to a pretty case of gold-digging?" he asked suddenly, and
the color crept under her pale skin, but before she could
reply he had walked away, and she gazed after him, the
old dislike back in her eyes. His words could have been
another warning or merely a derisive reminder that he had
not, in spite of a closer unity, revised his first opinion of
her.

He was right of course; she was no match for Roma,
whatever the odds. She could only accept the older girl's
pleasantries as she did the veiled snubs with the knowledge
that she and not Roma was the interloper, that however
much Astrea used her as a goad, Roma Nixon was secure
in the old allegiance, secure even in the knowledge of her
one-time power over Marc, to hurt him again if it suited
her, or to take, this time, that which she had once wantonly
thrown away.

"You mustn't take Astrea too seriously," she told
Charity indulgently. "She's given to fancies, you know."

"So everyone tells me."

"If, by everyone, you mean Marc, he's only trying to
warn you. Astrea's turned your head a little, perhaps, with
all this talk of money and adoption. You may even have
thought she had Marc up her sleeve for you as well."

"That's absurd!"

"Isn't it? All the same, honey, you could hardly be
blamed for cashing in while the going's good."

Charity looked at Roma, wanting to answer back, to

protest, even to hurl insults, but there was, she saw, no malice, then, in the older girl. Her attitude was one of wry amusement, she would, her manner proclaimed, do exactly the same herself, in Charity's place.

"Look," Charity said, trying to be reasonable, "I wish you would understand that I'm not in competition with you—over anything or anyone. It's all a little ridiculous, don't you think?"

"So long as you understand that, honey," said Roma with her warm, indolent smile. "I said you and I would get along, didn't I?"

It was, Charity discovered, only too easy to get along with Roma providing you gave in to her. Charity did not mind being made use of, but she found herself at the girl's beck and call far more than her employer's.

"Really!" Astrea exclaimed petulantly. "Dear Charity isn't employed as lady's maid. You should look after your own clothes, Roma, or employ a girl to do it for you."

"I couldn't afford it, Astrea, darling," retorted Roma serenely. "Besides, Charity doesn't mind, do you, honey?"

If Charity did mind, she was not going to admit it in front of Marc, who listened to such exchanges with a certain inquisitive humor and made no comment, but she wished Roma did not consider it necessary to repay her small services with gifts of unwanted clothing; they made her feel beholden in quite the wrong way and she never wore them. They lay in one of the drawers in her room, neatly folded, scarves, jumpers, even discarded lingerie, the faint perfume that clung to them an ever-present reminder of the donor.

"Why do you do it?" Marc enquired on one occasion. Roma never made any secret of her own generosity in such matters.

She shrugged and gave him a lazy look, quite aware that for some reason or other he did not approve.

"Well, I can hardly offer her money, can I?" she replied

carelessly. "After all, she's a cut above the usual little girl one finds in this kind of situation."

"One mightn't always think so, judging by your manner," he replied mildly, and she gave him a swift, calculating glance.

"Do I detect a rebuke, darling? She's hardly your cup of tea, I should have thought," she said.

"No? But then my tastes may have changed during the last seven years."

"Very possibly, but you don't convince me that the fastidious Marc Gentle can't do better than his aunt's paid companion."

"How you do harp on that aspect," he said with faint distaste, and quite suddenly the temper he remembered of old flared up.

"You're like Astrea!" she exclaimed. "You both enjoy rubbing in the virtues of that whey-faced little waif as a reminder of my own shortcomings."

He regarded her with interest and a certain admiration. Roma had always looked magnificent when driven to anger, and he smiled as he rememberd how his own coolness had always provoked a further outburst from her.

"Why do you smile?" she demanded then. "Do you enjoy getting your own back after all this time?"

"Not at all," he replied equably. "If I smiled, it was possibly at the rather absurd notion that you could be jealous of someone you describe as a whey-faced little waif."

"Jealous—of that poor little drip!"

"Your aspersions grow in picturesqueness, if not in accuracy, my dear."

"I'm not casting aspersions!" she said scornfully. "The poor girl can't help being plain, I suppose." He merely raised his eyebrows, and for a moment her anger was submerged in genuine curiosity. "Don't *you* think she's plain?"

"No."

Her eyes widened in disbelief.

"You're not going to treat me to that sad pierrot nonsense of Astrea's, are you?"

"I wasn't, no—though there is a slight suggestion at times; a certain plaintiveness, the traditional black and white melancholy, wouldn't you say?"

"I've never paid enough attention to the girl to notice," she snapped, and saw, too late, that he had simply been angling for a rise.

"Oh, Marc, you always enjoyed making me lose my temper," she said, reaching up her hands to her shoulders. "I think, perhaps, you still have a small weakness for me."

He looked down at the lovely face raised to his, and saw the first tiny lines of hardness and disillusionment round her mouth and eyes, and those infinitesimal flaws moved him more than her beauty.

"A weakness for you was once my undoing," he told her gravely, and her fingers tightened on his shoulders.

"Is it too late?" she asked softly, and when he did not reply, reached up to kiss him.

It was, perhaps, inevitable that Charity should interrupt them at that moment. The small study which had been made over to Roma as a sitting-room was virtually a passageway between two larger rooms and one or other of the household must frequently pass through it. She stood awkwardly in the doorway, uncertain whether to proceed on her way or go back and shut the door, and Roma snapped, without drawing away from Marc:

"Can't you knock if you want to come through here?"

"I—I'm sorry," Charity stammered. "I didn't know—I didn't think—"

"You didn't think Marc and I might like privacy upon occasion? Well, now you do know."

Charity's eyes went to Marc, and the coolness of his regard stung her to indignation and a curious, unaccustomed feeling of pain. He stood there quite unembarrassed, and his faint smile was a little mocking.

"You should," she told him, without pausing to choose her words, "hang a *Do Not Disturb* notice on the door for these occasions. I apologize for intruding."

She crossed the room with her nose in the air and went out by the other door, and Roma gave a soft little laugh.

"*Well!* I believe she has the beginning of a crush on you, darling—poor little scrap!" she said before the door was properly closed, and only then did Marc disengage himself.

"You enjoyed that, didn't you?" he said.

"Embarrassing the child? I didn't notice that you were in much of a hurry to spring guiltily apart!"

"Perhaps," he answered mildly, "I hadn't a great feeling of guilt."

"Why should you? If I know Astrea she will have acquainted her second spiritual daughter with our past history, long ago."

"Oh, undoubtedly—but these things can be misconstrued."

"Well, does it matter?"

"Not at all—" he replied with cool indifference "—no, probably not at all."

BUT IT mattered a great deal to Charity. She had heard Roma's remark as she left the room and she felt suddenly raw and nakedly exposed. They would have laughed together after she had gone, and Marc, who had been so unperturbed, might have felt a little flattered. They would treat her, in future, with kindly tolerance, he because his male ego would be soothed by her presumed change of heart, Roma because in the knowledge of her beauty and the power she had once held over him, she could afford to be magnanimous. And was it true, thought Charity, fighting an emotion that had never come her way before, was it true that this sense of awakening was no more than the crushes the girls in the shop had experienced for film stars and television personalities? Was there no more than that to the shy sense of familiarity she had felt with him

when they had stood under the cherry tree on Easter morning and he had quoted Housman? Sentimental rubbish, she
told herself angrily. Had he not said, himself, that he tried
his quotations out on her because all poetry lovers liked an
admiring audience? It was unfair to remember that she had
worn a white dress that same evening because it was Easter
and the spring of the year, and he had looked at her with
tenderness and said softly:

" 'Wearing white for Eastertide . . .' "

She suddenly disliked him again very much, so that it
was not difficult, when next they met, to be stiff and off-
hand with him, to show him, she hoped, that, although he
might laugh behind her back, it could make little difference to her.

The days slipped by quickly enough, and soon it would
be time for Marc to return to London. He and Roma
motored frequently into Brighton, where, it was to be supposed, she found an outlet for her boredom. They would
return in the evenings, sometimes very late, to be avidly
quizzed by Astrea who alternately made arch innuendoes
or declared herself to be neglected. Roma, after these occasions, seemed relaxed and very sure of herself; it was impossible to tell from Marc's manner how the day had
affected him.

Astrea discussed them both endlessly, and Charity
listened in duty bound to many disclosures that were not,
she felt, intended for her ears. It seemed as if her life, like
Astrea's, must henceforth be centred in these two, and it
became exhausting to catch the prevailing mood, for one
moment Astrea would declare her dearest wish of seven
years ago was about to come true, and the next would con-
demn Roma as a heartless mercenary who, even now,
would trifle with her nephew's affections, hoping that the
past might be forgotten.

"But she will not get my money!" she would exclaim.
"If she wants Marc, she must take him on his own terms,
as she would not years ago. You shall be my heir, dear,

dear Ganymede, my little cup-bearer. I have made that very plain.''

How plain she had made this nebulous statement Charity was still unsure; indeed she had become heartily tired of the subject. She had no wish to figure in Astrea's will, and it was not pleasant, she found, to be used as a threat to someone else. Roma had made her own interests fairly clear, Charity thought, and that was her business; if she wanted Marc as well then that was her business, too, but on this last reflection Charity wavered. Did he deserve nothing better than to rate as a meal ticket for someone he had once loved, and still did, for all she knew? It did not occur to her that Roma's affections might be seriously engaged, for had she not thrown him over, when it suited for a rich man old enough to be her grandfather? Oh, well, thought Charity crossly, serve him right, either way! He was disagreeable and superior, and, most, likely, cold as stone. She was unprepared, consequently, when on the last day of his visit he proposed that they should walk again to Cleat Beacon.

"It's raining," she said rather blankly.

"Good spring rain," he replied imperturbably. "Are you afraid of a mild soaking?"

"Of course not, only—"

"Only nothing. Go and change your shoes—you can't avoid me for ever, you know."

It was an unpromising remark. He had not, until now, appeared to notice that she had been avoiding him, or to show any particular desire for her company. It would be like him, she thought, obediently changing her shoes, casually to refer to that scene she had interrupted between himself and Roma, even to chide her mockingly for an imaginary interest in him. He would, she reflected sourly, be very good at nipping a supposed and unwanted infatuation in the bud, and Roma's expressions as she watched them set out did not encourage her to imagine there was any other object in the walk.

Up on the Beacon the wind and the rain drove against their faces in good earnest, and it was not until they turned back that conversation became possible. Even then Marc seemed preoccupied, and when he did speak it was only to point out some subject of interest in the countryside. Every so often he glanced down at her with an absent smile, and presently, when the rain became more than a spring shower, he drew her into the shelter of a chalky hollow in the breast of downland.

"You look a proper little scarecrow, Charity Child," he told her with a grin. He wore an old felt hat tipped over his eyes, but she had come bareheaded and the wet hair straggled over her forehead, sending little rivulets of water down her face.

"Well," she said prosaically, forgetting the object of the walk, "it's a good thing my hair is straight. At least I don't have to worry about the set of my perm."

He glanced at her affectionately.

"You have very little vanity in you, haven't you? It's rather an endearing trait," he said, and she looked surprised.

"I would have imagined you'd prefer a woman who took pride in her appearance," she answered primly.

"Would you? But there's a deal of difference between vanity and taking pride in one's appearance."

"I suppose so."

She answered cautiously, thinking of Roma, but it did not occur to her that he could make any comparison between them. She knew she was plain; until now it had never mattered very much.

"I think I would like to be nice-looking," she told him naively, and he frowned.

"That's a meaningless description of anyone," he exclaimed. "Beauty perhaps, quality certainly, but nice looks, never! It has an insipid sound."

"It's better than being just plain, surely?"

"And what makes you think you're plain, Pierrot?"

She looked up at the unexpected note of tenderness in his voice, then quickly away again. She did not want to revive that unfamiliar sense of intimacy with him, or to be drawn into dangerous personalities in this sheltered, lonely spot in the downs.

He said quite suddenly and in the same tone of voice:

"Did you catch Roma's last remark that day in the study?"

She caught her breath sharply, remembering that had always been a trick of his when he brought her up to the Beacon; to lull her into a false sense of security, then drop whatever bombshell he had in mind quite unexpectedly.

"Yes," she answered, too honest to evade the question or purposely misunderstand the occasion to which he referred.

"A pity," he said, and she rushed heedlessly into speech.

"It wasn't true . . . I was very embarrassed . . . I wouldn't want you to imagine . . . "

"I don't imagine—at least not many things," he said and, taking her by the shoulders, turned her gently round to face him. "I thought that was why you were avoiding me so politely. Did you imagine I'd pay any attention to that kind of remark except, perhaps, to regret that it wasn't true?"

"Regret?" Her eyes were dark with astonishment. This whole conversation was, like a dream, proceeding on incalculable lines.

"Why do you look so surprised? Men have their vanities as well as women—though, of course, we agreed that you have very little. Whatever you may have thought, I didn't care much for your earlier hostility, Charity."

"You started it," she retorted like a quarrelsome child. "You made your dislike and suspicion plain the moment you set eyes on me! Can you wonder that I felt hostile?"

"No, it was a most reasonable attitude," he replied with

a twinkle. "In fact it might also be said that your hostility allayed my suspicions. If you'd been the little schemer I thought you, you would have tried to placate me. You're refreshingly honest, my dear."

Her eyes filled with sudden tears. She was not honest, she thought desolately, aware now that Roma's spiteful observation had at least been true in essence. He could not know that, of course, neither could she fight Roma with her own weapons, for they would never be in her armoury.

He touched her wet lashes.

"Have I upset you?" he asked. "Was it too early to hope for a change of heart?"

His words, she thought, might be taken any way, for his tone was almost casual and she had no experience to fall back upon.

"I don't know how to answer you," she said unhappily, and he drew her wet head against his breast for a moment.

"No, I suppose not," he said. "And perhaps I'm not very sure what I'm asking. But I'm going away tomorrow, and I'd like to think that when I come back you will have grown a little fondness for me."

"Fondness?"

"Well, liking, then. There could, I think, be a seed of great liking in both of us."

Now she only wanted to run from him before she could offer him what he might not really want. Had he quarrelled already with Roma, she wondered, that he must seek solace or assurance from the nearest girl to hand?

He must have seen the doubt and bewilderment in her face, for he smiled a little wryly.

"I haven't made myself at all clear, have I?" he said.

"No."

"Well, don't let it worry you—we are only at the beginning of things, you and I."

"Are you and Roma—" she began, despite herself,

because that picture of them kissing in the study kept returning, but his expression immediately changed and the old mockery was back in his face.

"There's an adage that says 'never apologize, never explain.' It's worth following, I think. The rain has stopped; we'd best be getting back," he said, and that, thought Charity, silenced, was as far as one would ever get with the enigmatic Marc Gentle.

CHAPTER SIX

SHE THOUGHT Roma greeted them with relief when they got back to the house. She and Astrea had probably got on one another's nerves, shut up together on a wet afternoon, and Astrea's demands could prove a little exhausting. Charity did not miss the swift, enquiring look the girl sent Marc, and when her eyes finally came back to rest on Charity's bedraggled appearance she gave one of her slow, satisfied smiles.

"What a sketch you look, honey!" she said with pleasure. "Don't you go for those nifty little raincoats and hats in this country?"

"I like the rain on my head," Charity answered, still glowing from that strange, sweet intimacy on the downs. Roma must have been aware of some change in her, for her eyes suddenly narrowed.

"Not attractive to the opposite sex, my dear," she said sharply, "or did Marc pay you compliments?"

"As far as I can remember, I called her a scarecrow," Marc said, but there was an unaccustomed warmth in the smile he gave Charity.

Roma's mouth curled in amusement, but Astrea was immediately up in arms.

"Scarecrow, indeed!" she boomed, clasping the very wet Charity to her bosom. "My little Ganymede is one with nature—all Aquarians are free as air and so, so *simpatica*. Do you not find her *simpatica,* dear boy?"

"I wouldn't know," Marc retorted with a grin. "We

aren't, perhaps, on those terms. Hadn't the child better go and change?''

"Yes, yes, do that, dear child! Put on that pierrot frock with the toby frill—it becomes you so well—and, later, you shall play us *Au clair de la lune.* Roma, you smoke too much. You will ruin your health, besides which you will smell of the saloon bar.''

"Really, Astrea!" Roma murmured, and closed her eyes. Yes, thought Charity with a certain sympathy, it had clearly been a trying afternoon.

Charity put on the dress for which Astrea had asked, but she had no great liking for it. It made her look too thin and reminded her of the occasion when Marc's eyes had quizzed her unkindly in the candlelight and silently accused her of exploiting his aunt.

"Well!" observed Roma, viewing the frock with indulgent amusement. "I can't say I share dear Astrea's enthusiasm for your creation—it makes you look like a bean-pole!"

"You could not carry off such a simple gown, dear child," Astrea told her somewhat waspishly, and Charity sighed. It distressed her when Astrea singled her out for favors, for she only did it, she was sure, to pay back some imaginary grievance against the other girl.

"Your dress is beautiful," she said shyly to Roma, and saw Marc grin. It was, she supposed, annoyed with herself, a gauche attempt to divert their attention to Roma, but she had been sincere in her compliment. She admired all Roma's clothes.

"You can have it if you like," said Roma carelessly. "I'm sick of it, myself."

Charity flushed, aware that the offer had scarcely been made out of generosity, but she answered politely:

"Oh, no, thank you, Roma, I—I could never wear anything like that. I haven't the figure."

Roma looked pleased, but Marc observed with a barely concealed yawn:

"When you two girls have finished throwing bouquets—or are they brickbats—at each other, we might talk of something else. Are you staying on indefinitely, Roma?"

His sudden question held a serious note and Roma fluttered her lashes at him.

"I hope so, darling—if Astrea will keep me," she replied, and stretched a hand in charming supplication to the older woman, but Astrea was not in the mood for anyone's playacting but her own.

"We shall see," she said evasively. "It will make extra work for Minnie and there are the *bills* to be considered. Stubbs never intended this house to be used as a hotel. He told me so frequently."

"But, honey," Roma said with her soft little laugh, "you're a rich woman! Why should you bother your head about bills?"

"Because," retorted Astrea with surprising practicality, "that is the only way to *stay* rich. Stubbs had it all worked out. He started with a little liver and lights shop in the North End Road, Charity, dear child, and look where he ended!"

"Where did he end?" asked Charity, fascinated.

"Strings of sausages all over Sussex—all over England!" said Astrea, jingling her many charms with vague gestures in all directions.

Astrea's discourse upon the source of the Stubbs' fortune seemed to restore the atmosphere to normality. Marc did not pursue his enquiries as to Roma's future plans, and Roma herself, if not entirely back in favor, made more effort than was usual to flatter her hostess into good humor.

Listening to them sparring across the dinner table, Charity sat silent and thought about Marc. "We are only at the beginning of things, you and I," he had said, and that sounded somehow like Easter and the promise of new life . . . "Was it too early to hope for a change of heart?" he had said, and she had answered him foolishly because she did not know what reply he expected or if, indeed, a reply was expected at all . . .

"You're not eating, Charity," he remarked, and she found his eyes on her with the suggestion of a twinkle, as though he had known what she was thinking.

"Our learned friend, no doubt, upset her on their walk," said Roma, suddenly observant. "Did he give you a grilling, honey? He's pretty good at stripping away your defences, as I expect you've discovered."

It was intended, Charity thought, as a warning, or a possible reminder that she shared Marc's first suspicions that Charity was after Astrea's money; but the unexpected strangeness of that encounter in the rain was still with her, so that she answered simply, as if they were alone:

"Oh, no, he didn't grill me. He didn't even strip away my defences—perhaps there weren't any."

She saw Marc's eyebrows lift and heard the little irritable snap as Roma broke a roll in two.

"I wasn't thinking—I expect that sounded silly," she said nervously, and Roma frowned.

"I rather think it did," she said. "Marc, I shall be coming up to town sometime. Will you be able to spare me an evening?"

"Why not?" he replied, conversationally. "We used to patronize a very select night club off Berkeley Square, if I remember right."

"But you were no dancer," Roma reminded him with a small grimace. "Stiff and conventional and very proper."

"Proper?"

"We-ell . . . you had your moments, I'll admit. Oh, darling, we had some good times, didn't we?"

"Very good."

"And we can recapture that?"

"I doubt if one can recapture anything, Roma," he said with a smile, and she pouted and flicked a crumb of bread at him.

"We can try," she said, and in the candlelight her eyes were bright with invitation.

Charity sat and listened, marvelling at the ease with which they slipped back into a mood of the past. The things he had said to her on Cleat Beacon meant nothing after that brief, somehow significant exchange, and the picture of them kissing in the study came back as vividly as before.

"Did he give you a bit of a whirl in the rain, after all, honey?" Roma managed to whisper in her ear as they left the dining room. "Just keeping his hand in, so don't let it worry you any."

Charity felt angry with Marc, but most of all with herself. Why should he trouble with meaningless phrases when all he need have done was discuss the weather? Why should she, from the inexperience of a simple heart, read into his pleasantries something which was never intended? In the music room she sat as far away from him as possible and stared at him critically. His angular face no longer appeared attractive; his nose was too long, his eyes chilly, and he was years older than she—almost another generation—Roma's vintage. She was unaware that he was returning her regard until he spoke.

"You're scowling, Charity Child, and it doesn't become you. Is my face so repulsive?"

She jumped, conscious that he had focused attention on her again and, seeing the sudden glint in his eye, she would not have put it past him to have read her thoughts once more.

"I'm sorry," she said awkwardly. "I didn't mean to stare."

"Didn't you? What about this entertainment my aunt promised us?"

He was, she thought, embarrassing her on purpose. He had never been particularly interested in Astrea's musical evenings, and Roma was frankly bored by them. She shook her head dumbly, but Astrea rose delightedly to the bait.

"Play, dear child, play!" she cried, clapping her hands, and finished rather vaguely: " 'Music when soft voices die . . .' you know."

Charity could not refuse without drawing more attention to herself, but she sat down at the piano feeling like a child who had been bidden to please its tolerant elders. She began to play a Scarlatti study because she thought they deserved a lesson in discipline, but Astrea stopped her.

"No, no!" she protested shrilly. "Play *Clair de lune* and then the little French thing. Wait! I will place the light so—it will be the moon shining down upon you—and now you will see the likeness to Pierrot, Roma, dear child."

Marc watched with tender amusement, well aware of Charity's embarrassment. She had no notion of self-dramatization, poor child, he reflected with fondness. She sat on the stool, stiff and correct like a schoolgirl, and the likeness to Pierrot had gone, for she had withdrawn outside the meaning of the music, but as she drifted into the familiar nursery jingle, just for a moment the likeness came back.

> *"Ma chandelle est morte,*
> *Je n'ai pas de feu . . ."*

She had lifted her face in the lamplight and, suddenly, it was all there; the plaintive brows, the lost white face, the black etching of hair and toby frill . . . As she stopped playing he became aware of Roma's eyes watching him with cold calculation and saw her bite her lip.

Astrea applauded with her usual exaggeration and Roma stretched her arms above her head in indolent grace.

"Very nice," she observed to no one in particular. "I reckon that nursery rhyme stuff isn't difficult to rattle off."

"Simple things are always the most deceptive, dear child," Astrea reproved her. For a moment Roma's eyes flew wide open, then she relaxed and reached for a cigarette. Astrea was not subtle; she had probably meant exactly what she said, but there was a disturbing expression on Marc's face which showed that he had taken the point.

"What about a highball?" Roma drawled.

Marc straightened his tall body preparatory to mixing the drinks, but Astrea frowned.

"It is an unbecoming habit in a woman to drink whisky," she said. "In my day we were toasted in Imperial Tokay, or Napoleon brandy and, of course, pink champagne."

"Oh, come off it, Astrea!" exclaimed Roma, who had had enough for one evening. "You'll be telling us next you drank it out of slippers!"

"The gentlemen did that, dear child," replied Astrea, unabashed. "Oh, yes, many were the pairs of slippers I had ruined by champagne. Of course" —with a pointed look at Roma's feet— "I took size three—sometimes even *two*—such a pretty way it was of showing up other prima donnas' blemishes."

Marc burst out laughing.

"You're really very naughty, Astrea," he said. "I'd trust my eccentric aunt to have the last word anywhere. Here's your whisky, Roma; we'll be civilized, I think, and drink it out of glasses."

It had, thought Charity, undressing for bed, been an uncomfortable evening all round, and she hardly knew if she was glad or sorry that Marc was leaving in the morning. He and Roma had sat up talking after the other two had gone to bed, and on her way back from the bathroom, Charity heard them in the hall, talking in low voices, making dates, perhaps even kissing as they had in the study that day. She went to bed feeling hurt and bewildered; they took her up and then set her down and she did not know where she was with any of them. The next day Roma made it very plain.

"I THINK," she said when Charity brought up her breakfast tray, "you and I had best have a little talk."

"Now?" asked Charity with a sinking heart. She did not care at all for the look in Roma's eye.

"No, honey. I like my breakfast in peace and quiet. Come back mid-morning and help me move my things to my own room."

"Do you mean my room?"

"That's what I said, only you see it was never yours. Paid companions don't expect the best bedroom in the house, do they?"

"I only went where I was told," said Charity stiffly.

"Sure you did. But Astrea couldn't know then that the original spiritual daughter was returning to her bosom, could she?"

"I suppose not. I did offer to change, if you remember."

"So you've reminded me. Well, I'm going to take you up on that right now, so go and get the drawers and cupboards emptied."

"Very well," Charity said, "but—does Astrea know about this?"

"We'll tell her afterwards," Roma replied cosily. "No need to disturb the poor old girl before she's got her face on, is there?"

"No, but—she doesn't like her plans altered without being consulted."

"I ought to know that better than you, honey. I lived

here before. Now, hop along and make a start, and don't
go running to Madam with tales before we get going.''

''I shouldn't dream of it,'' said Charity gravely, and left
the room.

It did not take her long to put her few possessions
together, but Roma's wardrobe would be another matter.
There was certainly more space here, but even so, one of
the cabin trunks would have to remain, spoiling the
elegance of the room. Charity moved all her belongings on
to the landing when the time came and went to tell Roma
she was ready.

A few garments had been flung carelessly on the bed,
but otherwise Roma had not troubled to sort out her
things. She sat at the dressing table in a long jade-green
housecoat, making up her face, and waved a hand carelessly
towards the bed.

''Make a start, will you? I'll be along in a little while.''

Charity made several journeys between the two rooms
before Roma was ready to help. Even then she did not
trouble to dress but went vaguely backwards and forwards
with odd pieces of clothing, the housecoat trailing behind
her with a small whispering sound, and soon she gave up
carrying anything, but sat in an easy chair watching Charity
dispose of her clothes in cupboards and drawers, and
smoking incessantly.

''You know,'' she said suddenly, ''you should keep to
your proper place in this house if you want to stay.''

Charity kept her back turned and resolved not to lose
her temper.

''I think my proper place is Astrea's concern. She hasn't
complained,'' she said.

''Oh, Astrea's a silly old hay-bag who can be flattered
into anything. It amuses her at the moment to play you off
against me.''

Charity turned, really shocked to hear Astrea described

in such terms, but Roma was smiling and flicking ash unconcernedly on to the carpet.

"Don't look so disapproving, honey," she said. "I'm very fond of the old girl, but she's still a foolish, eccentric old woman who should be protected from her own folly."

"If," said Charity patiently, "you are still harping on the will, you might just as well forget it. I don't want her money and I don't suppose for a moment she's done anything about it."

"No? Well, we'll see—but I warn you, Charity, I'm up to all the tricks of little girls like you. Oh, don't think I blame you for trying, honey. It isn't nice to be poor and a girl must root for herself these days."

"Is that meant to be conciliatory?"

"Conciliatory? Well, you might put it that way, I suppose. In our different fashions we're after the same thing, which creates a fellow feeling in a way, but I told you very early on if your ambitions clashed with mine it would be just too bad."

Charity went on placing clothes on hangers, feeling the fine materials slip through her fingers with caressing luxury. It did not seem to her that, living in such different worlds, her ambitions could ever clash with Roma's. She turned round slowly, trying to find words which might end this needless antagonism.

"Roma—" she began hesitantly. "I wish I could make you understand that all this is—is so unnecessary. I'm paid to do a job here, as you've pointed out. I don't expect to—to make something out of it. You say I should keep to my proper place in the house, but I can only do what's required of me by my employer."

"Including running after your employer's nephew?"

The color crept under Charity's pale skin.

"What do you mean?" she asked quietly, and Roma gave her soft little laugh.

"Oh, it wouldn't surprise me if Astrea had put you up to that, too," she said. "The new spiritual daughter scoring off the old."

"That's quite absurd!"

"Yes, isn't it? As if Marc would look twice at you!"

The temper was rising in Charity. She wanted to strike that insolent face, so arrogant in its own beauty, so sure of power over others.

"Have you finished?" she asked.

"No, I haven't," Roma answered, and her indolence suddenly left her. "You should know for your own good what men say about girls who chase them. Oh, I daresay our learned friend made a mild pass or two up there on the Beacon, but you invited it, didn't you? Marc's a man of the world, and doesn't expect his polite attentions to be taken seriously, but you embarrassed him by running after him and making your poor little hopes so plain. He told me so, himself."

"Marc said that?" Charity had gone very white, and Roma lit another cigarette and inhaled the smoke luxuriously.

"Sure he did—last night when you'd gone to bed. I doubt if he'll be coming down next weekend in consequence."

"I see." Charity turned back again to the cupboard to hide the bitter tears which sprang to her eyes. She felt physically sick, remembering them whispering in the hall, and all the magic of the rainy afternoon had turned to shame. Behind her, she heard Roma's voice talking on and on.

"Well, honey, I've had my say. I don't suppose you liked it, but the truth is seldom pleasant. I don't advise you to run to Astrea for sympathy, because she can be so very unpredictable, and however tiresomely she's behaving now she always wanted me to marry Marc, as I expect you know. I don't say he may not have turned to you for solace for a sore heart, for I'll admit I treated him badly, but now—well, things didn't pan out for me, so I'm willing to settle for the old love. Be well and truly warned, my dear Charity, I mean to get the money, and Marc, too. I can't say fairer than that."

Charity whirled round, her hands covering her ears.

"Oh, stop, stop!" she cried. "You don't have to go on any more. You're welcome to Marc and the money and anything else you can get, only—don't hurt him, will you?"

Roma looked at her curiously and, for the first time, saw what a man might find to attract him. There was a defencelessness in Charity which begged for protection, a passionate simplicity which cried out for love and the privilege to give with both hands. She was not plain, this thin, ardent child, and she possessed the priceless gift of being virgin soil.

"You really are fond of Marc, aren't you?" Roma said slowly. She had never been made aware of a selfless spirit before.

"Yes—no—I don't know," said Charity distractedly. "Whatever it is, it was delicate and scarcely born, and you've killed it, and for that I won't forgive you."

"Oh, heck, who cares!" snapped Roma impatiently. "You don't need to put on an act with me, you tiresome brat—Astrea's histrionics are enough for one household."

As if on cue, Astrea herself swept into the room. Like Roma, she was still in the process of getting dressed and the old négligé she affected in the morning trailed its torn lace over the carpet.

"What is the meaning of all this clutter on the landing, Charity, dear child?" she boomed. "Are you spring-cleaning your room, by any chance?"

Charity was beyond speech at that moment, and Roma

got out of her chair in one graceful movement and put an arm round Astrea's shoulders.

"Now, darling, don't be annoyed," she said coaxingly. "We decided to change, that's all. My lovely room that you furnished specially for me—Astrea, honey, I couldn't bear not to have it any longer, and Charity, very sweetly, said she didn't mind, so *you* won't, will you?"

Charity watched them through her tears. Roma's lightning change of mood filled her with grudging admiration, and she waited, almost with indifference, for Astrea's reaction.

"I was not consulted," Astrea replied, but the familiar note of outrage was muted today. She looked very old and not too well, and her wrinkled, painted face showed up in the morning light in cruel contrast to Roma's flawless beauty.

"You had no right—" she began again. "This is my house and I give the orders. You, dear child, are only visiting here."

"Visiting?" Roma's husky voice was rich with a simulation of love and warmth. "Astrea, I've come home! Whatever the past I've come home to Cleat—and to you darling."

Astrea's eyes grew moist and she swayed a little for an instant.

"Ah, Roma . . ." she said. ". . . my dear, dear child . . . my true spiritual daughter . . . But Charity must not feel hurt by this," she finished in her usual strong tones, and became aware then of Charity's tear-stained face. "You have minded, my child? Then it shall not be! You will change back at once, Roma—at once, do you hear me? You have not cared for my broken heart for seven years—why should I now care for yours?"

"Oh, really, Astrea, you're impossible!" snapped Roma, her patience suddenly breaking, and all at once they were shouting at one another. It was, Charity supposed, what they had been accustomed to do in the past, but coming on top of that other scene, it was too much.

"Oh, please, both of you!" she implored, trying to come between them, and one of Astrea's gesticulating hands caught her inadvertently on the side of the head.

"Oh, my child, my poor, poor child, I struck you!" Astrea wailed, halted in full flood, then she clutched at her breast with a little cry and her face contorted in a spasm of pain.

"Astrea, what is it?" cried Charity, alarmed, but the reply she got was incoherent and unintelligible, and with a small sigh, the old diva fell heavily at her feet.

IT WAS Minnie, hastily summoned, who procured order out of chaos. Charity was frightened by Astrea's bad color and heavy breathing, and even Roma had gone a little pale. It was immensely comforting to be rated by Minnie and watch her unperturbed measures for reviving her mistress.

"Ought to be ashamed of yourselves, shouting and bawling for all the house to hear!" she snapped. "I've been expecting this for a long time with all her carryings on. Drop dead one of these days, she will, getting herself all worked up as does. Miss Roma, you're the strong one—lend me a hand to prop her up."

"But what is it? What's wrong with her?" asked Charity, watching anxiously while Minnie and Roma between them heaved Astrea into a more comfortable position.

"Just a little collapse—she's had 'em before. Her heart's none too good and she isn't as young as she was."

"You mean she's had a heard attack? I didn't know there was anything wrong with her," Roma said thoughtfully, and old Minnie looked up for a brief moment and sniffed.

"Don't be counting your chickens yet, Miss Roma," she said caustically. "Madam will be all right. As to not knowing, what should you know of her health, gadding in America all these years and barely a letter home?"

"Oughtn't we to get a doctor?" Charity asked, not caring for the swift calculation she saw written in Roma's face, but Astrea was coming round.

"No doctor . . . Minnie knows what to do . . ." she murmured weakly.

"But, Astrea—"

"Save your breath," Minnie snapped. "She won't have 'em, and there's no need this time, anyway. Noakes is working somewhere in the garden. Run and fetch him, Miss Charity, and we'll get her to bed."

Astrea was still confused. Charity, as she ran out of the room, heard her say: "I struck you, Roma, my poor child . . ." and Roma replied softly: "You didn't mean it, darling . . . I understand. . . ."

When Charity visited her much later, she seemed to be almost normal, propped up in bed in her own room, grumbling at the old dresser's ministrations, fresh makeup disguising the drawnness of her face.

"Does Marc know about these attacks?" Charity asked.

"No, and he's not to," returned Astrea sharply. "I can trust you, I hope, dear child. Roma has already given me her promise."

"Very well," replied Charity a little dubiously. It was, she supposed, no concern of hers to meddle in the affairs of a family in which she had no place, but her personal concern for Astrea was very real.

"I wish," she said earnestly, "you'd see a doctor. I—we are all so anxious for you."

"I'll see a doctor when I have to and no sooner. Find Roma for me, dear child. I struck her; I must make amends."

It did not seem worth while to undeceive her, and Roma obviously, was taking advantage of the mistake. During the two days when Astrea kept to her bed, it was Roma who was repeatedly sent for and who spent long hours in the sick-room with a gentle patience quite foreign to her nature. She was, Charity supposed, cashing in, to use her own expression, on Astrea's sudden change of heart. She did not grudge the girl her rightful place in the house; she could only hope that Astrea would not see through her and be hurt all over again.

How much pain for so little reward, she reflected, going dully about her own affairs, and her thoughts would return to Marc and she would wonder if, perhaps, she fretted too much. She knew so little about him when all was said and done, and the tenderness she had discovered beneath that hard exterior could have been imagined. In the end Roma would have no power to hurt him because they were, perhaps, two of a kind.

"You look peaky," Minnie declared, giving Charity a shrewd look. "Been worrying about m'lady?"

"Yes, I have."

"And other things too, I shouldn't wonder. Well, I'll say this for you, young miss. I didn't take to you at first on account of them others, but you've proved me wrong. You've got heart."

"Heart . . ." Charity's voice lingered sadly as she echoed the word, and Minnie gave her customary sniff.

"Too much, I shouldn't wonder," she observed. "Lost it to Mr. Marc, have you, ducks?"

"No!" said Charity with vehement distaste, before she realized that to be addressed as "ducks" by Minnie was mark of her approval.

The old woman just smiled and said, "Ah, well . . ." and pattered back to the kitchen.

When Astrea was up and about again, Roma spent

several days in London, returning with new clothes which Astrea had presumably paid for. She seemed in great humor and was looking radiant.

"Did you see Marc?" Astrea asked. She had been fretful during Roma's absence and seemed to have lost much of her old zest for life.

"Of course, darling. He sent his love and said he would be down next weekend. He was sorry about last time."

"Press of work—he told me." Astrea sounded indifferent.

"A useful excuse and possibly true," Roma replied with a sidelong glance at Charity, and later, when the two girls were alone, she said with kindly assurance:

"No need to be shy of him when he comes, honey. He perfectly understands."

"Understands what?" asked Charity, feeling suddenly cold.

"Why, that you'd allowed yourself to get a little foolish over him. He's very sorry if he gave you any cause to get wrong ideas."

Charity had been living in an unnatural kind of vacuum for too long and her healthy emotions now came bubbling through.

"How dare you discuss me with Marc!" she exclaimed, her eyes bright with anger. "How dare you—or Marc, either—stick me on a pin like an insect and—and examine my emotions?"

"Well, really, my dear, I was only trying to be helpful," said Roma, rather taken aback. "Anyone would think, to hear you talk, that you'd *really* fallen for the guy."

"And if I have, then it's you who's made me see it," said Charity, the true state of her heart revealing itself clearly for the first time. "But don't worry, Roma; I may not know my proper place, but I've no intention of throwing myself at a man who doesn't want me."

"I'm glad to hear it," was all the other girl could find to say, but her eyes were suddenly wary, and when she was alone with Astrea she tentatively suggested that Charity should be found another job.

"No, no," protested Astrea at once. "She's a good child, a kind child. Where would she go?"

"But she can't have expected to stop here for ever, and now I've come home where's the point of a companion?"

"You will marry and leave me again—oh, yes, I know you mean to get Marc."

"That's another reason," Roma said, evading the issue for the moment. "Poor little Charity's rather lost her heart to Marc. It would only be kind to let her go."

"O-ho! So you want her out of the way?" said Astrea, who missed very few tricks of this kind. "I confess I had toyed with the idea of her for Marc—so good for his ego—you would never pander to it. I have another little scheme, dear child. The money for you and the dear boy for Ganymede. How would that be?"

"Not at all suitable, Astrea darling," said Roma, lowering her heavy lids. "But, talking of the money, have you seen your lawyers yet?"

"No," said Astrea a little peevishly, "the stars were not propitious."

"But don't you think you should, honey? That little attack you had the other day—well, one never knows, does one?"

"Later, dear child, later," Astrea replied irritably, and Roma, who seldom overplayed her hand, left it at that. She had found out what she wanted to know. No will had yet been made in favor of Charity, and, with a little judicious juggling with the stars, she should be able to guide Astrea's mind into the right channels.

When Marc came down at the weekend, he caught Charity totally unprepared. She had gone for a walk to the

Beacon to be out of the way when he arrived, and had never expected to see his tall figure climbing the track to meet her. In this moment of watching him, all her brave resolves seemed to melt away and her bones turned to water, so that when he reached her and took both her hands in his, she could only leave them there and gaze at him speechlessly.

"You're looking fine-drawn. Aren't you well?" he said, examining her critically.

"Quite well," she answered. "And you? You look tired."

His smile was the old mocking one she remembered.

"It must be a mark of progress that we each first look for well-being in the other," he said, and quite suddenly he pulled her into his arms and kissed her.

"Oh . . ." she said, then again, "Oh . . ."

"Be quiet, Pierrot," he murmured against her mouth.

The April wind blew merrily about them and, somewhere near, young larks chirruped in their hidden nest in the grass. His cheek was warm and hard against hers, and his hands suddenly gentle on her shoulders.

She opened her eyes after what seemed a lifetime, then broke from him and fled precipitately down the hillside.

CHAPTER SEVEN

ROMA'S EYES missed very little where her own interests were concerned, and one look at Charity's revealing face as she ran into the house and up the stairs confirmed her suspicions that Marc's attention had possibly begun to wander.

"It's too bad of you," she told him softly as he mixed her a drink before dinner that evening.

"What's too bad of me?" he asked with a smile. "That I had to cancel our last dinner date on account of work?"

"Oh, that! Of course not, darling—our other dates made up for it, didn't they?"

"You were always a glamorous person to take around. You still are," he told her gracefully.

She took her whisky and raised her glass to him.

"Good fortune!" she said. "I will always wish you that, Marc, and it looks like coming true, doesn't it? You have quite a reputation at the Bar, so I'm told. The shekels must be pouring in."

His smile was a little wry.

"Are you having regrets on that count, my dear? It doesn't always pay to be hasty in your judgments, you know."

Her eyes grew soft and melancholy.

"I've learnt that," she said with a sigh. "I've learnt a great many things in the past seven years."

"Life was disappointing, in spite of the dollars?"

"Yes. They didn't bring me comfort—or love."

"Do you need comfort, Roma?"

"I need love."

"The two can mean the same, I think. I discovered that some time ago."

"You? But you've never married."

"Not so far." He cocked an eyebrow at her. "Now tell me what's too bad of me."

She remembered that irritating forensic habit of returning suddenly to a point which had not escaped him, but this time she was pleased with the opening.

"Too bad of you to give that little companion of Astrea's inflated ideas of herself," she said, and saw the instant masking of those familiar features.

"If you're alluding to Charity, I suggest we leave her out of the conversation," he replied coldly. "She has nothing to do with us."

"Of course not, darling, but do you think you're being quite fair?"

His eyebrows lifted, but he made no reply, and she went on, stretching deliberately so that the lovely lines of her body were clear and inviting.

"You've made the odd pass at her, honey, haven't you? I can't say I admire your taste, but men see their women differently, I suppose."

A little nerve in his cheek twitched convulsively.

"That's not a very pretty thing to say," he replied with the icy reserve of temper held in check.

"I daresay not, but the girl is very young. She probably likes to boast that the brilliant Marc Gentle has designs on her."

"Is that what she's told you?"

"Of course. She couldn't wait to brag that you had chased her up to the Beacon this very afternoon as soon as you arrived. You shouldn't play with paid employees, darling; they're all alike—kiss and tell."

"Thank you," he said courteously, but there was a pinched whiteness about this nostrils that warned her not to pursue the conversation, and she was relieved that Astrea chose that moment to join them and demand her usual glass of sherry.

Charity slipped into the room as late as possible, and Astrea remarked a little peevishly:

"You are frequently late these days, dear child. You disappoint me. Have you said good evening to my nephew?"

"We've already paid our mutual respects—on Cleat Beacon," Marc said rather grimly, and at the amused look of satisfaction on Roma's face, Charity felt herself beginning to blush.

She blushed so painfully that all their eyes were upon her. Roma gave her soft little laugh and Marc observed with cruel deliberation:

"What a charming picture of guilt! Do you have other assignations on the Beacon, by any chance?"

She could not reply, for her shame was too deep. He had been discussing her with Roma again, and they had laughed and, perhaps, made unkind jokes. She wanted to run from the room as she had run from Marc on the Beacon, because there was no comfort any more, no warmth, no love. Minnie mercifully rang the gong and they all went in to dinner.

All through the meal Marc deliberately ignored her. Roma played, perfectly, the daughter of the house making gracious small talk, but Charity's enforced silences seemed to annoy Astrea.

"What is the matter with you, child?" she kept demanding impatiently. "If you are not well, you should say so and go to your room. I expect a companion to be just that—*companionable*. You are a disappointment to me. Perhaps, after all, you are too young for the post."

"Don't bully her, Astrea," Roma said with light reproach, adding to Marc in just the same tone:

"You aren't helping much either, darling. It must be very dull for Charity having to listen to family affairs in which she has no part."

"Really?" he said, giving Charity a brief, casual glance.

"Of course. To be employed in a household like this must be a very tricky proposition, but now I've come home again, there's no real need for Astrea to employ a companion, is there? Did I tell you, Marc, I went to hear you in court the other day? You were magnificent—and how that wig becomes you!"

"Really?" he said again, and suddenly turned to Charity.

"Will you walk to the Beacon with me again tomorrow?" he asked with a sudden savage inflection, and her eyes slid away from his.

"No," she said. "No, I don't think so."

"Then we might as well go to the coast, Marc," Roma said, with an inviting twist to her full red mouth. "It's spring and—you and I have got a lot of leeway to make up."

"Why not?" he answered smoothly and, to Charity's relief, the meal was suddenly ended.

It was not difficult to keep out of his way for the rest of the weekend. She stayed in her room, forgoing breakfast, until she heard them setting out for Brighton in the middle of the morning, and when they came back in time for dinner, Astrea monopolized the evening with anecdotes and record playing, and a rather pathetic effort to recapture the spirit of those other evenings and her past successes.

"Will you play, dear child?" she asked Charity when the evening seemed to pall, but Charity could not have played, with Marc still treating her with the contempt he must feel for anyone who had run after him, and Roma, relaxed in her chair like a surfeited cat, sure in the knowledge of her own power.

Her apologetic refusal caused a mild storm.

"Really!" Astrea exclaimed with a coldness that was quite foreign to her. "I sometimes wonder what you think you are here for, dear child. I house you and treat you as my own—and all the time this dear child, Roma, was waiting to bring comfort to my old age. Is it too much to ask that you should play for me? After all, it's that for which I employed you, is it not?"

Marc looked at Charity. Her face was the face of a bewildered child, a child who had suddenly too much to bear and was nearly at breaking point. He was angry with her, and bitterly disappointed, but he did not want to watch that sad clown's face much longer.

"Leave her alone, Astrea," he said unexpectedly. "She's tired, I think. You shouldn't expect us all to have your amazing resistance and vitality. Let the child go to bed."

The tears sprang to Charity's eyes at this unlooked-for rescue and she scrambled awkwardly to her feet.

"If you will excuse me, Astrea," she said, and made her way, thankfully, out of the room.

She was so tired that she stumbled on the stairs and instinctively made for the room which had once been hers, but, on the threshold, she turned away, remembering. Roma had resumed her control of the house, of Astrea and of Marc, too. She would go away, she thought, wearily, away from this semblance of comfort and warmth and affection, back into the world which offered none of these things.

She took a bath in spite of her tiredness, hoping it would make her sleep, and, on the way back to her room, ran straight into Marc. The lights in the house had been put out and he was, presumably, on his way to bed. She would have passed him quickly, without speaking, but he stretched an arm across the passage, resting his weight on the wall and blocking her path.

"Well, Charity Child, do you feel better for your ablutions?" he asked.

"Yes, thank you," she answered, and stood waiting patiently for him to allow her to pass.

"You," he said in suddenly soft accents, "are the misguided little girl who kissed and told. Did no one ever teach you the ethics of these matters?"

She blinked up at him in the dim light. His face was the face she remembered the day he had first met her at the station, cold and forbidding, and sharp with suspicion.

"I don't understand," she said.

"Don't you? I'd thought more highly of you, Charity, than to go bleating to Roma, of all people, of my unwelcome attentions. You didn't, I must confess, show any very great reluctance up there on the downs."

She only stared up at him, too tired to take in what he was implying, too sick at heart to care very much. His eyes flicked over her. She looked absurdly young in her long blue dressing-gown, the damp hair clinging to her well-scrubbed forehead, a spongebag clasped to her chest. Her natural defencelessness brought back again the old urge to shake or kiss her.

"Are you really just one of these silly little girls who like to boast of a conquest?" he asked, and when she did not reply, took his hand suddenly from the wall and stood aside to let her pass.

"Goodnight, Pierrot," he said mockingly, and she replied, because she had suddenly found herself forced back to their first encounter:

"Goodnight, Mr. Gentle. I—I don't suppose you will be coming down next weekend?"

"Oh, yes, I shall be coming," he said with a certain sardonic relish, and watched her slight, suddenly vanquished figure disappear down the passage to her room.

Monday morning brought its usual backwash. Marc was late getting off owing to a late breakfast because one of the daily women failed to turn up, which also put Minnie in a bad temper; the butcher sent chops instead of cutlets for lunch, and the scullery sink became blocked. They were all things which, strangely enough, helped to boost Charity's sinking spirits, for it was comforting to find that such minor disasters could befall a rich household as well as a poor one, and when her father had been alive, these mishaps had been everyday occurrences. She walked to the village to change the chops, and even managed, with Noakes' help, to free the sink; it was discouraging, therefore, to be summoned by Astrea and rated because she had not been available to carry out her daily duty of reading aloud the forecast of the stars in the daily newspapers.

"What do I pay you for, dear child?" demanded Astrea crossly. "You have always been so *simpatica* about the forecasts. At this stage of my affairs the rulings of the planets are *most* important."

"I'll read them now," Charity said, without stopping to make excuses, but Astrea waved her away.

"Do not trouble," she said grandly. "This dear child has already done so."

Charity looked at Roma, sitting so smugly by Astrea's bedside, and her suspicion that Roma's reading of the stars would conform with her own desires was answered by the indolent amusement in the other girl's face.

" 'A day for seeking legal advice and making decisions,' " quoted Astrea, jingling her charms. "Ring up my lawyers, please, Charity, and ask Mr. Fenimore to come down here."

Charity felt a wave of anger and, uncaring how her action might appear to Roma, began to read for herself the forecasts for Virgo in the pile of papers on the bed. Most of the advice was vague and meaningless, but here it was in one of them. *A day for seeking legal advice and making decisions* . . .

"You see?" said Roma, watching her face with malicious enjoyment, and Astrea suddenly rounded on Charity.

"Were you doubting Roma's honesty?" she asked, and her fingers trembled a little as she pushed them through her dyed red hair. "You disappoint me very much."

"No, Astrea," Charity replied gently. Roma was clearly working to put her in the wrong, but she could not speak the truth without bringing distress to the old lady.

"Very well, then, go and ring them up, and don't bungle the appointment," Astrea ordered, still with displeasure, then added, sounding suddenly very tired: "Roma is right. It is time I put my affairs in order."

"You're tired—why not wait another day?" said Charity impulsively, but Astrea stretched out a beringed hand to feel for Roma's.

"Another day may be too late," she said with her old love of drama, then at Charity's startled expression she laughed a little unkindly.

"Don't think I'm going to die yet, and don't think I've already altered my will in your favor and want to change it again," she said querulously, and Charity left the room without replying and went downstairs to telephone.

"You shouldn't try to antagonize her," Roma said later. "I can always persuade her to leave you a tiny legacy. Minnie will be down for something, so why not you?"

"Please don't trouble," Charity replied with distaste. "Minnie has been with her for nearly forty years and it would be scandalous if you tried to influence Astrea to cut down her legacy—but I am quite a different matter. I've been here only three months."

Roma gave her a look of dislike.

"You've dug yourself in pretty well in such a short time, haven't you, honey?" she said disagreeably. "Astrea—even the fastidious Mr. Gentle coming to heel. Well, I think your duty is about over, Charity Child. We're all of us wise to your little tricks, now."

Charity regarded her with that grave stare which Roma found disturbing.

"Roma," she said, trying to speak reasonably, "I don't like you any more than you like me, but I do beg you to be careful how you deal with Astrea. She's not well, for all her denials, and I think that little heart attack was more serious than Minnie let us believe."

"My dear girl, why should I trouble myself to dislike you?" retorted Roma insolently. "I'm even a little sorry for you, though I confess I find your—er—insinuations a shade impertinent. After all, you're just the paid companion here."

Charity blinked

"You're very fond of reminding me of that," she said quietly. "I think you must be a bit old-fashioned. A paid companion, these days, is not a servant."

Roma's glance was uneasy. She did not want to drive the girl into awkward revelations with Astrea or, more dangerous still, with Marc.

"Of course not," she said hastily. "I'm sorry if I've given that impression, but I find you difficult to place."

"It's very simple," Charity said. "'I'm just a girl, like thousands of others, who has to earn my living as best I can, but that doesn't give you, or anyone else, a reason for treating me like dirt."

Roma looked up swiftly at the unfamiliar note of condemnation and even contempt in the younger girl's voice. Was the dumb little cluck daring to criticize her?

"I'm not aware you have been treated like dirt at Cleat," she retorted viciously. "On the contrary, Astrea has spoilt you ridiculously and given you inflated ideas—

so, evidently, has our learned friend, who's doubtless regretting it."

She saw the pain and defeat in Charity's eyes at the mention of Marc, and her confidence was restored. She had, it was evident, successfully scotched that little incident.

"Well, honey," she said more amiably, "we'll just have to put up with each other for a while. I don't imagine you'll be staying long now there's no need for Astrea to employ a companion."

"Are you definitely making your home here?"

"Until I marry again."

"I see."

Charity, indeed, saw more than she liked. She could not grudge Roma her rightful place at Cleat, but her tender heart ached for the old prima donna who would never know the difference between affection and exploitation; even for Marc Gentle, caught once again in the toils of an old infatuation, and prepared, it seemed, to barter reality for illusion. Did men only desire what seemed unattainable, she wondered sadly, for Marc, she knew, was not like Astrea. He was too intelligent, too wordly-wise not to recognize Roma for what she was. This time, he would take her and expect little in return, and that, thought Charity, was dead sea fruit.

MR. FENIMORE'S appointment to visit Cleat was for Friday, but that same morning his clerk telephoned to express regrets that, owing to a sudden chill, the old gentleman would be unable to travel down to the country. Astrea was inordinately put out, more for the disappointment of postponement than any urgency in the matter, but Roma added fuel to the fire by insinuating that Charity might have had a hand in the matter.

"I wouldn't put it past her," she said. "She tried to dissuade you at the beginning, if you remember, darling. She could easily have put the old boy off, herself."

"But why?" demanded Astrea. "I am not ill—it can only mean a postponement."

"A postponement is always a help if you hope to benefit," Roma said, and the old eyes clouded.

"Nonsense!" she exclaimed, and Roma stooped to give her a light, airy kiss.

"It isn't nonsense," she said with soft reproof. "You yourself had already given her the idea she was to inherit. You can't blame the girl for being alarmed when I unexpectedly come home to cut her out."

"I haven't," retorted Astrea, stung, as always, by opposition, "said you will cut her out. You neither of you know my intentions, and, after all, what gratitude did you show, Roma, dear child, running off with that old man? If you had waited—"

"If I'd taken Marc, as you wanted, you mean? But Marc was stubborn. He wouldn't have conditions attached to our marriage."

"And you wouldn't take him as he was—do not forget that."

"I know, honey—I was flying too high, and I paid, for look at me now—not a cent, no home but yours, and the wasted years behind me."

"Got found out too soon by your old Yankee husband, did you? Ingratitude brings its own punishment," said Astrea smugly, and Roma's mouth tightened. Her patience with the old lady's vagaries was beginning to wear thin.

"Ingratitude is what you usually get for foolish indulgence of a dependant," she said crisply. "Has Charity fooled you with her soft speech and gentle ways? For all your kindness to her she thinks you treat her like dirt—nothing better than a servant—she told me so."

"Like dirt—my little Ganymede?" For a moment Astrea's eyes held the hurt astonishment of a child's, then her outraged indignation boiled over.

"It's too much!" she cried. "She's no better than all the

others—indeed she is worse, for I trusted and loved her.
Marc was right at the beginning, and I should have listened.
Roma, my dear, dear child, you were sent to me in
time—my true spiritual daughter to save me from that
other. She shall go at once—no, at the end of the month,
for I must not be hasty, and the child will have nowhere to
go. Send her to me, now.''

Roma hesitated, torn between satisfaction that she had
so easily achieved her own ends and doubt at the advisability of precipitating a crisis on the eve of Marc's visit.
Astrea was always unpredictable, and Charity, if she
chose, could make a good case out for herself.

"Why not leave it till after the weekend, darling?'' she
suggested. ''We don't want tears and scenes while Marc's
here, do we?''

"Charity has never made scenes, she is *simpatica*,''
Astrea rebuked her. ''No, no, dear child, I must be guided
by the stars. I have been warned today and the message is
quite clear. Send her to me.''

Charity, if saddened by the interview, was not surprised;
it had been plain for some time that Roma meant to get her
out of Cleat, but her heart was heavy at the nature of her
dismissal. She did not understand the import of many of
Astrea's accusations, for her reasoning appeared more
confused than real, and it seemed futile to deny the twisted
half-truths which could so clearly be traced to their natural
sources. She wept a little, not, as Astrea supposed, in
penitence or remorse, but because she had come to love the
old diva with all her whims and eccentricities, and was loth
to leave her unprotected.

"You weep, my child?'' Astrea said, at last exhausted by
her own histrionics. ''Perhaps I may reconsider. You are,
after all, so young, and you have not meant to hurt me, I
think.''

"No, I have never meant to hurt you,'' said Charity,

also exhausted. "I'm grateful and I love you, Astrea, but I will go at the end of the month just the same. It will be better so."

"It is the first of May tomorrow. You cannot go at once. What do the stars foretell today? Oh, Roma told me . . . 'you are surrounded by false friends; be strong and make a clean break . . .' "

Charity picked up the newspaper, which was still open at the column set aside for the stars.

"That's the reading for Libra. It comes directly under Virgo. Roma must have made a mistake," she said quietly.

"A mistake? Then what is the reading for Virgo?"

" 'A day of no importance; you should watch your health . . .' "

"My health . . . yes . . . send Minnie to me, will you, dear child?"

Charity looked at her sharply. The correct reading of the day's forecast was quite sufficient to put fresh ideas into Astrea's head, she knew, but the old lady did not look well. She could not stand the scenes she so delighted to make as she used to before that last attack, and, when Minnie came, the girl's unspoken enquiry was anxious.

"Now, ducks, what have you been up to?" the old servant said, as if to a child. "Getting yourself in a state because that old lawyer chap couldn't come down today? Miss Roma says she'll take you up to London next week to see him in his office, though where's the hurry after all this long time beats me."

"There may be hurry, there may be," said Astrea with sudden urgency. "My stars say I must watch my health today."

"Those dratted stars!" snapped Minnie. "What do you want to read 'em to her for, Miss Charity?"

"I won't be doing it much longer, Minnie," Charity replied. "I shall be leaving soon."

"Leaving?" echoed Minnie sharply. "Had enough of us already, just when you might be of use?"

"It's Madam's wish," said Charity wearily, and Minnie sniffed.

"Miss Roma been getting at you again, ducks?" she said. "Never did know the false from the true, did you?"

"Surrounded by false friends . . . surrounded by false friends . . ." murmured Astrea vaguely. "The stars said that, too."

Minnie compressed her lips, but only settled her mistress more comfortably and ordered her to take a strong dose of her heart medicine.

"Take no notice," she muttered to Charity. "She'll doubtless change her mind again—usually does."

But Roma would see to it that there was no change of mind this time, Charity thought, and in her heart knew that it was best. She had no place here at Cleat any longer, and she could not wish to stop on week after week or even month after month and watch the development of Roma's carefully laid plans.

Marc was not expected until the evening on Saturday, but he took the household by surprise by arriving at Cleat before luncheon. Astrea, who still did not feel very well, was staying in her room until dinner time, and Roma had hired the car from the village and driven into Brighton to shop, so only Charity was there to greet him, and she thought with dismay of the meal they must partake of alone together in the gloomy dining room, and the long, solitary afternoon ahead.

"Well," he observed, surveying her evident reluctance for his company with sardonic amusement, "you'll have to put up with me for the time being. I promise to keep my distance."

It was unkind, she thought, to remind her immediately of past mistakes, but she had never deluded herself that the weekend would be easy or pleasant.

"I'd better tell Minnie you're here," she said awkwardly. "She won't have anything prepared as there was only me to cater for. Are you content with bread and cheese?"

"Why not? Or, better still, I'll take you out to lunch and so avert Minnie's grumbles," he replied, and seemed to be enjoying her obvious embarrassment. He cut short her protests with his customary brusqueness and told her to go and do something to her face and be quick about it. He would, in the meantime, go upstairs and pay his respects to his aunt.

"Well, where shall we go?" he said when they were settled in the car. "Brighton and a slap-up lunch with obsequious waiters and discreet music? No, I don't think so—you don't look right for the phoney splendors of tripperdom."

"Am I not suitably dressed?" asked Charity nervously. When Roma visited Brighton she wore mink, outrageous heels and jewels. Charity had put on a plain dark dress and sandals and, because the day was warm, had no coat or hat or gloves.

Marc gave her a careless glance and grinned. The prim white collar of her high-necked frock made her look rather like a schoolgirl.

"Why so anxious?" he said with a hint of mockery. "You are very suitably dressed, Charity Child. No man would dare to take advantage of you in that confection."

Charity sighed. It was, she saw, going to be a matter of fencing between them, of disconcerting remarks on his side and the half-bitter raillery at which he was so expert. She would, she thought, keep silent when possible, and she hoped that luncheon would not be too much of an ordeal.

He drove down Cleat Hill and through the village and on into the wooded Weald which she had never been able to explore, and as the car moved leisurely through the twisting Sussex lanes, dappled with sunlight, she could forget her silent escort and relax. The woods had a misty softness pierced by the fresh green of larch and the delicacy of silver birch. An old countryman working at his hedging and ditching waved them by with a nod of greeting, children ran out of cottage doorways to shout, and the small gardens were a riot of color with aubrietia climbing over banks and walls.

They stopped in a village with a green and a pond and a beautiful seventeenth-century inn. A maypole was set up on the green, gay with its many-colored twisted streamers.

Marc said, "Well, will you care about this, do you think? The pub has quite a reputation for plain country fare. It's worth a visit, anyway, if only for a mug of beer."

He got out and stretched his legs, screwing up his eyes against the sun which struck dazzling light from the pond. He was not, Charity knew, really consulting her wishes; he had chosen, before they started, where he would lunch.

She followed him across a small paved courtyard and into the raftered hall of the inn. The cross-beams were thick and blackened with age, and burnished copper pans and brasses hung on walls which had yellowed with smoke. There was no one there but themselves, and Marc fetched drinks from a tiny bar in one of the alcoves and set them on a table, beer for himself in a pewter tankard, and cider for Charity. She did not like to refuse, remembering how her protests had always provoked him to mockery, but the cider was unexpectedly pleasant and cool and she drank it with enjoyment.

He watched her curiously over the rim of his tankard. She drank like a child, carefully holding the glass in both hands, and he observed how slender her hands were, long and delicate, the fingernails unpainted.

"You have nice hands," he remarked, and her eyes went to his own hands, strong and nervous, and she remembered how he had thrust them into his pockets, unable to control them the day Roma came home.

The thought provoked a chain of others: Roma's face

lifted to his as they kissed, the loveliness of Easter morning
and the flowering cherry tree against the sky; Roma, sure
in the strength of her beauty, commanding him, inviting;
the bitter-sweetness of that first and only kiss on Cleat
Beacon—Roma taking it all away and cheapening what
had been the innocent beginnings of wonder . . .

"You haven't much to say for yourself, Charity Child,"
Marc observed. "Am I a bad host, or are you merely a
reluctant guest?"

She jumped guiltily, and catching in the sudden quizzical
tenderness of his expression the quality which had charmed
her from her first dislike of him, her bruised spirit cried
out against the ending of so much felicity.

"Did your aunt tell you I'm to leave Cleat?" she asked,
and saw his sudden frown.

"No. Have you been sacked?"

"I suppose so. She doesn't need me any more, now
Roma's come back."

His eyebrows rose in two considering arcs.

"My aunt will, doubtless, change her mind," he observed
dryly. "She's given to whims and fancies of the moment."

"Oh, yes, I know, but I shall go just the same. It's best
that way," she said, and did not know how stretched and
wide her eyes seemed in her white face, nor how dark and
puzzled the plaintive brows.

"Poor Pierrot," he said gently. "I warned you you were a
new toy. When do you go?"

"At the end of the month—four weeks from today, I suppose."

"May Day . . ." he said, seeming to drift away from the
subject as if he were not very interested. "Do you know that
in certain parts of the country this day had great
significance? In Cornwall they still have the Hobby Horse
and the Mummers and the ritual of dancing through the
streets. Even here, as you saw, there's a maypole and

children will dance on the green. We may see some of it before we leave."

"Is that why you brought me here?" asked Charity, thinking what a strange, unpredictable man he was.

"Perhaps, " he said with a smile. "Finish your cider, Charity, and we'll go in to lunch."

The little dining room was dark with its low-beamed ceiling and latticed windows. There was an open grill where a white-capped chef turned a joint on a spit and cooked steaks and chops to order; the tables were few and widely spaced, and only one other couple were in possession, just finishing their lunch.

"How lovely—how different," Charity said, her eyes round, like a child's.

"Has no one ever taken you to little places like this?" he asked, he picked up the menu. "I think you would be fun to take around, Charity Child, if you could forget to be so proper."

"Proper?"

"Well, shall we say, defensive? You've changed, you know. You've lost that composure that used to worry me in the days when I bit your head off. Relax, now, and enjoy the very good steak that will be prepared for us—or would you rather have lamb or the roast beef of old England and Yorkshire pud?"

But it was not easy to relax with the fastidious Marc Gentle sitting opposite, discussing with explicit exactness the timing of steaks with the attentive chef, and procuring with accustomed authority other delicacies that were not on the menu at all. It was not surprising, she thought, that she had lost the composure which indifference had brought. Every so often he would look across at her, with a wry lift of the eyebrow, as if he found her unrewarding company, and she was plagued by the feeling that he thought her unappreciative.

"You know," she said, because so much of the day was puzzling her, "I've never thought of you in places like this."

"Haven't you, Charity? But perhaps you haven't thought of me at all," he answered, but she knew he was getting at her. From Roma's observations it was evident he imagined that she thought of him too much.

"I imagine you in smart London restaurants—with glamorous women," she said quickly, hoping to hide her gaucheness, but his grin told her that he accepted this for what it was, the unconsidered statement of an inexperienced young girl.

"You don't know very much about me, do you?" he countered, and she replied, without thinking:

"No—except that, perhaps, you have waited too long."

That startled him.

"What a strange remark," he said and, before she could try to retrieve a comment so unconsidered, began to quote softly:

> " 'Spring will not wait the loiterer's time
> Who keeps so long away;
> So others wear the broom and climb
> The hedgerows heaped with may , . .'

Is that what you meant, Charity?"

"Housman again—how you do love him," Charity said, and all at once things seemed as they used to be. The guard that she must put upon her tongue could be forgotten, and he was again the companion of her solitary dreams, the man who, like her father, could guess at her immature thoughts and shape them to reality.

"Is that what you meant?" he persisted, but she would not be drawn into so intimate an analysis of her reflections. She had been thinking of Roma, but she could not trespass in the unknown territory of his desires.

"I spoke without thinking," she said. "Say some more from *A Shropshire Lad* for me."

"*Say* some more? Why don't you ask me to recite and have done with it?" he mocked with a wry little smile, but he obeyed, nevertheless, selecting quotations at random, lulling her into a state of quiet content until he asked suddenly:

"What made you tell Roma I had kissed you?"

She was jerked back to reality by the harshness in his voice. Had he brought her here, after all, only to rate her, or, worse still, to remind her, in person, that no man cared to be pursued?

"I—I didn't," she stammered, not understanding why he should ask such a question.

His shrewd eyes flicked over her, alert and penetrating, and she felt as she knew his victims must feel in the witness-box. She could almost see the ghostly outline of a wig framing his angular features, the wig which Roma had declared to be so becoming to him, then his mouth suddenly lost its hardness in a small, ironic smile.

"Oh, I see," he said with an enigmatic inflection, and immediately spoke of something else, but, for Charity, the brief moment of respite had gone. She could only see him now through Roma's eyes, the man who would one day marry her with or without love, the man who had philandered elsewhere in an idle moment and regretted it.

They had been late with their luncheon and the other couple had long since gone, but they lingered over their coffee, for Marc seemed abstracted and disinclined to move. Presently the sound of the village band from the green told them that the May Day dancing had begun, and Marc called for his bill. They stood for a time with a group of villagers watching the dancing, but there was no magic in it for Charity. The children were unskilled in their manipulation of the maypole ribbons and not very attractive in their rather ill-fitting white frocks; the band played with apathy and out of tune, and a dogfight started on the edge of the green.

"Come on," Marc said impatiently. "The canine impromptu act is obviously going to be a bigger attraction than the dancers. Let's leave them to it."

It was only in keeping with the day that the maypole festivities should have been a failure, thought Charity as they drove away, but as they came again to the wooded lanes which had so pleased her, Marc pulled into a little clearing and switched off his engine.

"Well, Pierrot, shall we walk in the wood?" he said, with a lifted eyebrow.

Charity obediently got out of the car. She could not imagine why he should want to prolong an occasion which had scarcely been an unqualified success, but to make excuses would only have implied that she did not trust herself to him.

As she began to walk down the narrow path which led into the wood, his voice behind her observed with that disconcerting habit he had of reading her thoughts:

"You see I am keeping my distance, as promised. What a ridiculous waist you have, Charity. What does it measure?"

"I don't know," she said nervously, and felt him suddenly pull at her belt to halt her progress.

She stood there stiffly, wondering if he was going to kiss her again, despite his conviction that she had been chasing him, but he only gave her a gentle prod and let go her belt.

"Go on," he said. "There's a fallen log over there in full view of the road. We might, with impunity, sit there for a bit and enjoy the spring sunshine, don't you think?"

THE LOG lay across the mouth of a clearing in the wood and was overgrown with moss and lichen. Charity perched

at one end, carefully smoothing her skirt and feeling a little
foolish; Marc sat astride the log at the other end and suddenly burst out laughing.

"How very naïve you are, Charity Child," he said.
"Very naïve, and rather endearing. Did you know this part
of Sussex used to be famed for its iron foundries a century
or so ago? You can still see the old hammer ponds in the
woods."

"Can you?" she said politely, and sat picking at the
cool, green moss between them. She could not follow his
alternating moods and she wished, suddenly, that she
might wander off alone and explore. Bluebells, almost
over, made a carpet of blue through the trees and the
branches of young, unfolding breech were a delicate pat-
tern against the sky.

"Where will you go when you leave Cleat?" he asked
her abruptly.

"I don't know. It depends what sort of job I find, I
suppose."

"And what do you imagine you're fitted for? Will you
go back to thumping a piano in the Charing Cross Road,
or will you try to find another eccentric old lady like my
aunt?"

His voice was mocking and she thought the implication
was plain. He was still, it seemed, unconvinced of her intentions where his aunt was concerned.

"I don't know," she said again. "I haven't had time to
think."

"No? Do you remember I once told you I was beginning
to suspect you were marked out for disappointment,
disillusionment and, probably, grief?"

She sent him a startled look.

"Yes," she said. "You told me, too, that I had no
business to get myself born into this day and age. What did
you mean?"

"Don't you know? You're an anachronism, poor, lost

Pierrot—perhaps we both are. Well, you've experienced the disappointment—even the disillusionment. I trust, so far, grief has kept away.''

He was speaking lightly, even flippantly, but her spirit ached afresh, for grief had not kept away; grief ran through her numbed thoughts now as it had done when her father had died.

"Oh, yes," she answered with bright hardness, "grief has kept away, thank you. What is there to grieve for?"

"What indeed? As our friend Housman would have it:

> '*Ay, she lies down lightly,*
> *She lies not down to weep . . .*'

Do you never weep, Charity? But of course you do. I've seen you."

She was ready to weep now, at the heartlessness she found in him, at the piercing sweetness of the spring day.

"It isn't very gallant to remind someone of past foolishness—*any* sort of foolishness," she retorted, suddenly goaded beyond endurance. "Why should you care if I weep? Why should you care what becomes of me?"

"Oddly enough, I do," he replied with mild rebuke. "I have a slight feeling of responsibility, since Astrea is my aunt. Would you consider marrying me?"

She stared at him speechlessly for a moment. The expression on his face had in no way altered, and he flicked a beetle fastidiously from his coat sleeve as if his extraordinary question had no importance.

"*What* did you say?" she asked, then.

"You heard. After all, one job is as good as another, I should have thought."

The sun went behind a cloud, leaving the wood dim and unfriendly and suddenly chilly. She said, because the thought was uppermost in her mind:

"But you are going to marry Roma."

"Does she say so?" he enquired with lifted eyebrows. "Roma seems to spread a lot of false ideas, one way and another. You'd better take me, Charity Child; we would be protection for one another."

Anger suddenly mounted in Charity, consuming the hurts Marc and Astrea had dealt her, and the mischief Roma had made.

"I *will* not be a bone of contention between you and Roma, or a—a whipping post, or—or a safety valve for you!" she cried incoherently, and saw him smile.

"What an odd assortment of metaphors," he observed mildly. "Are you a bone of contention, Charity?"

"I always have been!" she stormed at him. "First between you and Astrea, then between Astrea and Roma, and now—now you offer this—this *monstrous* suggestion because you have a slight feeling of responsibility and need protection from another woman!"

He regarded her thoughtfully and with much interest.

"Dear me!" he said reflectively. "I do seem to have been clumsy. I had no idea that an offer of marriage might be considered monstrous."

"Of *course* it's monstrous!" she exclaimed, nearly in tears. "You imagined, I suppose, a p-proposal was expected because I ran after you—because you *thought* I ran after you, I mean."

"Did Roma tell you that, too?"

She had sprung to her feet at her first outburst of temper, feeling at an advantage looking down at him, but now the rage began to seep away, leaving only misery.

"Wasn't it true?" she asked; then, without waiting for a reply, she leapt over the log and ran, weeping, into the wood.

He did not follow her, and she wandered about for a long time, trampling down the bluebells, running blindly into branches that stung her face and brambles which tore at her dress. Like everything else that day the wood proved to be an illusion; it petered out quite suddenly in a disused rubbish heap piled with tin cans and broken bottles. She laughed a little hysterically and began slowly retracing her steps.

Marc was still sitting on the log, gazing abstractedly at the sky, and the sun highlighted his nose unkindly, emphasizing its length. She advanced a little sheepishly, conscious of her scratched face and torn stockings, and he rose slowly to his elegant height and surveyed her.

"You look a trifle dishevelled. I fear they will assume the worst at home," he said. It was not a moment to tease, he supposed, but having bungled his approach, he could do nothing else but endeavor to relieve her embarrassment.

She said nothing, but stood there, staring at him with her great, drowned eyes. He was still a stranger, for she had no experience in matters of the heart to guide her, and no instinct as yet, to pierce the protective armor of another.

He took out his handkerchief and gently dabbed at a little trickle of blood on her cheek.

"So you've turned me down, have you?" he asked, and she moved away out of reach of his ministrations.

"Yes," she said with grave dignity. "For I think you were making fun of me."

"Do you? I can't share your sense of humor, I'm afraid. Wouldn't you have said, on that score, that Charity Gentle might be a happier combination than Charity Child?"

"No less silly," she said tartly.

He sighed and replaced the handkerchief in his pocket.

"Well, I suppose we'd better be getting home," he said. "It must be nearly tea-time."

He hardly spoke on the way back to Cleat except to point out marks of interest in the countryside. Whatever his object had been in making his ridiculous proposal, he seemed to be quite unmoved by his rejection.

Charity sat beside him, feeling a little foolish. She was

conscious that her own behavior had not been very dignified, but his had been beyond her understanding. She could only be grateful, she supposed, that in the end he had acted as he did, for had he followed her into the wood and taken her into his arms she would have been lost. Meagre satisfaction lay in the knowledge that now he would know that she had not been running after him, but she viewed the rest of his visit with misgiving; he had only to show tenderness for her proud defences to come tumbling down.

"Like the walls of Jericho," she said, forgetting that she had spoken aloud.

He gave a little smile as he changed gear for the steep rise of Cleat Hill.

" 'And it came to pass, when the people heard the sound of the trumpet . . . the wall fell down flat . . .' " he quoted.

She glanced at him uneasily, wondering whether she had revealed more of herself than she cared to, but he made no further comment, and soon they pulled up behind a strange car in the drive of the house. Charity was speculating with surprise as to who might be visiting, for callers were rare at Cleat, when the front door opened and Roma came running out. She still wore the smart clothes in which she had gone to Brighton, but her hair was carelessly set and her eyes red with weeping.

"Where have you been?" she demanded of Marc, her voice shrill with a mixture of alarm and suspicion. "Did you have to go joy-riding with Charity today of all days? Why weren't you *here*?"

Marc looked at her curiously. Perhaps for him, too, thought Charity, it was a new experience to see Roma stripped of her poise.

"If you remember, I wasn't expected until this evening," he replied coolly. "You weren't here when I arrived, so I took Charity out to lunch. Any objections?"

"Plenty," she snapped viciously, "but they can come later. It's Astrea. She's had a heart attack. She's unconscious and I think she's going to die." Her face crumpled into tears again and, even in her own sharp alarm, Charity found time to marvel that Roma should be moved to weeping.

Marc pushed past her without ceremony and went into the house and, when Charity would have followed, Roma caught her by the arm.

"The doctor's with her now. No need to hurry," she said. "We should get that lawyer down. I've tried his office, but it's closed Saturdays. Do you know his home number, Charity?"

Charity turned slowly to look at her, and she knew with sickening certainty that this, then, was the cause of Roma's distress; not grief for an old lady who might, at this moment, be dying, but a fevered fear that by Monday it could be too late for her inheritance.

"No, I don't," she said. "And if she's as bad as you think, it's no time to be troubling her with lawyers."

"Of course it's time! This business has been postponed and postponed. Now it may be too late."

"Isn't her peace of mind more important?"

"No! Don't *you* care, Charity? You may be mentioned in the will."

"No," said Charity and walked into the house.

It all seemed very quiet. Doors stood open to the rooms and the May sunshine spilled over Astrea's confused assortment of treasures; the hideous oriental press in the hall, the cabinets of glass and china and worthless bric-à-brac which filled most of the rooms, the Persian rugs of doubtful origin, the fine pieces of furniture which rubbed shoulders with the rest. How strange, thought Charity, surveying it all, how strange that these mute objects could represent a lifetime's tastes and fancies and, in the end, fall under the hammer, for there was nothing here that Roma would want, and only the miscellaneous contents of the music-room might catch the fancy of a musical collector, and so perpetuate her name.

"Charity"—Roma had followed her in—"something *should* be done about the lawyers. Can't you think? Astrea must have old Fenimore's home address somewhere. She was quite pally with him."

"Be *quiet!*" Charity said, her eyes suddenly anguished. The scent of the lilac which she had picked and arranged only yesterday came to her on a warm wave of nostalgic spring. For ever the scent of lilac and the old-fashioned wax polish that Minnie used would remind her of this first day of May when so much had crowded into her life.

Roma was regarding her speculatively. She had time, now, to observe the torn stockings, the pinched look of shock and control in the younger girl's face.

"*Well*—" she began in her accustomed husky drawl.

"Be quiet!" said Charity again, her eyes focusing with difficulty on the lovely, arrogant face which, even now, was ready to taunt her. "How bad is she?"

Roma shrugged. Already her first panic had passed. Sickness in the house was a bore, and it looked as if, this time, Astrea would be unable to dismiss her ills as of no account.

"It's hard to say," she replied indifferently. "The doctor seems to take a grave view, but he was a bit snooty at not being called in earlier. She's well over seventy, poor old girl, and in her heyday, hit the high spots quite considerably, I imagine."

"What brought on the attack?" asked Charity, and Roma's eyes shifted for an imperceptible moment, then returned to regard Charity with her customary tolerance.

"Oh, we had a little argument—nothing at all, really— but you know what Astrea is. She worked herself up into one of those frenzies of nonsense and, suddenly, she collapsed. It was like that time the other day, only worse. Minnie couldn't bring her round, and when she did, neither of us could lift her. If Marc had been here instead of acquainting you with the facts of life in the bushes, something might have been done more quickly," she finished viciously.

Charity let it pass. It no longer seemed important what Roma did or said, or even Marc. Astrea, that colorful personality of a bygone age, was upstairs, dying, perhaps. She was forgotten by all but the few, but when she went, a little of the panache of life would go with her.

"Has she asked for me?" she said, and Roma fumbled in the pockets of her elegant suit for a cigarette.

"Why should she?" she replied insolently. "You're under notice, so I believe."

It seemed a long time later that Marc and the doctor came downstairs together. They stood talking gravely in the hall, then Marc accompanied the stout little man to his car. Roma was lounging in her sitting room, the radio switched on to a program of dance music; Charity waited in the music-room, trying to escape the heartless beat of saxophone and drum.

"Turn that thing off," Marc ordered sharply when he came back into the house. "She might hear it in her room."

Roma obliged with a lift of the eyebrow, and Charity came through from the music-room.

"How is she?" she asked.

"She's regained consciousness, but that's about all," he answered grimly. She looked like a little ghost, standing there in the doorway, and his eyes softened.

"Go and get tidy, Charity Child," he said. "There's nothing anyone can do at present, and you don't need to sit about in laddered stockings, do you?"

"You should exercise more discretion when you make your passes, darling," Roma observed as Charity left the room, and he wheeled round on her.

"Do you have to persist in this cheap form of belittlement even when we've more important things to think of?" he demanded furiously, and she shrank back at the unfamiliar look of distaste in his eyes.

"Marc—I'm sorry—" she said softly. "I—I've been jealous, I know. You've only been trying to pay me back, haven't you? But I can still be jealous—even of a poor little drip like Charity Child. You see, I didn't know till too late what a fool I'd been seven years ago. Can't you understand?"

He took out his case to select a cigarette and absently offered it to her. The momentary anger seemed to have gone from him and he regarded her with curious abstraction.

"Every seven years one becomes a different being, haven't you heard that one?" he said. "One sheds a skin, or grows another—I forget which."

"And have you changed your skin, Marc?"

"I shouldn't be surprised. Seven years is a long time."

"I must have changed mine too, then. Marc—it isn't easy for me to be humble. Can't you forget the past and start again? I—I'll come to you on your own terms this time, no matter what Astrea decides about her will."

"I wonder," he said a little cruelly, "if you'd be so willing had all those dollars not been lost to you."

The color flamed in her cheeks and he remembered how easily he could provoke her temper.

"If anyone else but you had said that to me, I'd have spat in his eye," she said stormily, but he only smiled.

"If you'd any pride left you would have spat in mine," he told her amiably. "Your timing is bad, Roma. This is hardly the moment for staking a Grand Reconciliation scene."

She stubbed her cigarette out violently, and lighted one of her own.

"Oh, your British sense of decorum!" she exclaimed. "Can't I declare my feelings because your aunt upstairs may die?"

"I don't think it's really a matter of nationality," he replied mildly. "After all, you're English yourself, my dear, however much you like to cling to that fetching American accent."

"Is she really bad?" Roma asked, admitting defeat for the moment. "What did the doctor say?"

"He was, not unnaturally, slightly stuffy on the question of past attacks. Why didn't somebody tell me?"

"Astrea wouldn't have it. Besides, Minnie said it wasn't serious."

"Not serious—heart attacks!"

"Well, you know Minnie—guards the old girl like a lioness and is as stubborn as hell. How long does he give her?"

Marc's eyes were shrewd and attentive.

"You're thinking of the will, aren't you?" he said with deceptive gentleness.

"Well, naturally. Do you like to think of all that money going to charity—or have you, by any chance, got hopes for the other Charity?"

"I think we'll leave the other Charity out of this," he said quietly. "You've done enough damage, Roma. Let well alone, now."

"What do you mean?"

"You know very well, I think. You've distorted the truth and, where truth didn't exist, you've invented."

"Has Charity also been distorting the truth?" she asked unpleasantly, and he shook his head.

"You traded on that, too, didn't you?" he said. "Charity doesn't run from one person to another with tales, and you knew it."

Quite suddenly, she saw that all she had schemed for had slipped through her fingers, just as had those bright American dollars: all except her inheritance, and for that she would work, no matter what it cost, in the short time that might be left.

"You've changed, Marc," she said, on a little sigh. "There was a time when you would never have spoken to me like that—never compared me—unfavorably—with your aunt's paid companion."

"Yes," he agreed gravely, "but in those days, you see, I hadn't met Charity. I understand from Minnie, by the way, that it was the scene you made when you discovered I'd taken her out to lunch that precipitated Astrea's attack. Not very pretty, is it?"

"Oh, you're impossible!" she exclaimed violently, and suddenly slammed out of the room.

CHAPTER EIGHT

ALL THE next day they waited uneasily for any change. The doctor came and went, promising to send a night nurse to relieve Minnie, who would not leave the sickroom. There was, he said, nothing to be done. Astrea's valiant old heart was worn out; she might last indefinitely if she avoided another attack, or she might go out like a light.

It grieved Charity immeasurably that she was not allowed in the sick-room.

"Sorry, honey, but she's got a bee in her bonnet where you're concerned since that day she sacked you," Roma told her quite kindly. "In a little while, maybe, she'll be more reasonable, but you know Astrea! At the moment she won't let me out of her sight. Having a bit of remorse, I guess, at her true spiritual daughter being left in the cold for seven years."

"Yes, I see," said Charity unhappily. "But you *will* tell me if—if she should ask for me?"

"Sure I will."

"And don't—don't bother her about the will, or lawyers, or anything."

"Anything else, Miss Child?"

"No—just give her my love."

The day dragged slowly. The sound of church bells through the open windows reminded Charity of that other Sunday when she and Marc had walked to church together on Easter morning, but even Marc was not very clear in her mind just now. She busied herself with Minnie's daily chores, helped by the village women, who were ghoulishly enjoying the solemnity of a possible death in the house, and she only saw Marc at meal-times.

"You're taking this too hardly," he told her when, in the evening, he managed to persuade her to sit down in the music-room with a glass of champagne. "She may recover if she avoids another attack, the doctor thinks."

"She doesn't need me any more—she doesn't even want to see me," Charity said. "Marc—don't let Roma worry her about the will."

His mouth tightened.

"Even Roma wouldn't badger a dying woman," he said.

"Dying? But you said—"

"It was a figure of speech, but—we must be prepared, my dear. She's very old—a great deal older than she's always let on."

"Is she? I can't imagine her gone."

"You're very fond of her, aren't you, Charity?" he said with tenderness, and sitting down on the arm of her chair, drew her gently against him.

She did not, in that moment, think of him as the man she had hated, then loved and, finally, been humiliated by. She only knew that there was a great comfort to be drawn from him and that in some strange fashion he too might need comfort.

"You're like my father," she told him, resting her head against his shoulder.

His smile was a little twisted.

"Do you want me to take the place of your father, Pierrot?" he asked with a certain dry humor.

"No, not really. It's all quite different."

"I hope so. I've misled you sadly, I'm afraid."

"Misled me?"

"Yes. But you see I was unsure of you—I think I still am, for want of better encouragement. Perhaps I had already sensed this confusion with your father."

"Yes," she said, too exhausted to understand, and he gave her shoulder a little squeeze.

"You're very tired, aren't you?" he said gently, and suddenly Roma came into the room trailing filmy draperies and a cloud of scent.

"Well!" she observed with malicious sarcasm, "what a cosy spectacle! Champagne, too—are you celebrating something?"

Marc rose unhurriedly to his feet.

"The champagne is mainly medicinal; we've all been under a strain. You'd better have some, too," he said, and moved to the table to fill another glass.

"I could do with it," Roma said. She had clearly been to much trouble over her appearance when no one had thought of changing, and had entered the room with great buoyancy, but now she flung herself into a chair and took the glass Marc handed her with a tired little droop.

"I've been on duty most of the day," she said, yawning. "Poor old Minnie had to have some rest. She's not so young as she was."

"Minnie is as tough as Astrea. There's no need for you to wear yourself out," Marc said.

"Oh! Will you be going back to town tomorrow?"

"Yes, but I shall be down again in the evening."

"Oh," she said, again, and frowned. It did not suit her to have him around any longer. She had lost him, and that mealy-mouthed little miss should be made to pay, but Roma had always been one to cut her losses, and she had other fish to fry before it was too late.

"That should please you, shouldn't it, honey?" she remarked sweetly to Charity. "A man's sympathy is always easier to batten on, isn't it? Poor old Astrea won't have you at any price."

With a gesture so sudden and unexpected that it took both girls by surprise, Marc seized her roughly by the hand and pulled her to her feet. The champagne spilled down her lovely dress, but even Roma did not notice. She stood there dazedly with Marc towering over her, and Charity, appalled, thought he would strike her.

"Have you lost all sense of decency?" he said with dangerous calm. "Can't you stop your brawling and baiting for five minutes when a woman may be dying upstairs? If this was not my aunt's house I'd turn you out neck and crop."

"Who says she's dying?" said Roma defiantly, and at that moment the door opened and Minnie stood there, her old face puckered, her eyes red-rimmed and hopeless.

"What is it?" Marc asked sharply, and Charity rose to her feet with a sudden premonition of disaster.

"She's asking for Miss Charity," the old dresser said apathetically. "Been asking all afternoon, but Miss Roma made excuses. You did ought to go to her, ducks, even if she did hurt your feelings, giving you the push. She's sorry now."

"But I thought—" The blood rushed in a wave of color to Charity's face, and in a flash she was out of the room and they could see her long legs taking the stairs two at a time.

"Well," Marc said, stooping to pick up the empty glass which Roma had dropped. "One more of your charming tricks uncovered."

"Oh, go to hell!" snapped Roma, and poured herself another glass of champagne.

"Should have fetched young miss myself, I suppose, but I didn't like to leave Madam alone with Miss Roma," muttered Minnie, who had paid no attention to this exchange. "Always on about that dratted will, she was, and my poor lady wanting to sleep."

"It didn't, I suppose, occur to you," observed Marc, turning to Roma with the utmost calm, "that with a lawyer already under the roof it was scarcely necessary to panic so much about getting another?"

She stared at him stupidly, the champagne beginning to trickle over the edge of the tilted glass.

"But you're a barrister," she said.

"I'm still a lawyer. Really, Roma, for a woman of your sharp wits, you can be incredibly stupid at times."

"You mean you've already drawn up her will?"

"Oh, yes, this morning. She signed it and the doctor and Mrs. Who-is-it from the village witnessed it. You can relax now, Roma; there's nothing to be gained."

He pushed gently past Minnie in the doorway and went upstairs to his aunt's bedroom.

Charity, when she reached Astrea's door, knocked timidly and stepped inside. The room presented an unfamiliar appearance, tidied of its customary litter, and the vast ornate bed turned back to front with its foot pressed against the wall because Astrea had insisted that she might have been wrong about her theory of the magnetic north. The first warm promise of summer evenings drifted in at the open window; the sound of a mowing machine, the intermitten notes of bird-song dying with the fading light.

At first Charity could not see Astrea propped up in the bed, then a weak hand stretched out to her.

"Is that Charity?" she asked, and her voice sounded old and alarmingly frail, Charity moved swiftly round the high, draped head of the bed and took the old, wrinkled hand in both her young ones.

"Dear Astrea," she said. "I would have come before if I'd known you wanted me."

"My little Ganymede . . . my cup-bearer . . . they said you would not come because I was turning you away."

"Roma knew that wasn't true," said Charity steadily, and Astrea sighed.

"Yes, yes . . . she was jealous, no doubt. But she only wants my money . . . America has changed her . . . or perhaps it was my fault in the very beginning."

"It's easy to spoil those we love," Charity said gently.

"And Roma is so beautiful."

"I was like her at that age—do you find that hard to believe?" Astrea asked a little wistfully, and Charity smiled, her eyes filling with tears. Without the paint and mascara, the old face looked strange and oddly unfamiliar like the swept and garnished room; only the dyed red hair bore witness to that valiant battle with age. Astrea was just a tired old woman, no longer caring much that she had long since been forgotten.

"I have remembered—it was you I struck that day—not Roma," she said suddenly in a stronger voice.

"You were muddled afterwards. It didn't matter."

"But she let me think it was her. She accepted my contrition so charmingly, and all the time, my dear, dear child—"

"Astrea, it doesn't matter—in any case it was an accident."

"She would not have it so. She means to marry my nephew this time, you know. She will break his heart all over again . . ."

Charity had not heard Marc's footsteps on the thick carpet, and she jumped when she saw him standing there, tall and dark, on the other side of the bed.

"She didn't break it the first time, dear aunt. My heart is composed of pretty durable material as, no doubt, Charity would tell you," he observed a trifle grimly.

Astrea turned her head to look at him, pulling fretfully at the old, threadbare drapes at the head of the bed.

"You like to think you are impregnable, dear boy, but we none of us are . . . we none of us are . . ." she said, and sighed.

"No, my dear, but don't let it trouble you."

"Trouble—trouble! I had thought that you and my little Ganymede—but she wouldn't do, I don't doubt. You would walk over her."

"Oh, I don't think so," he replied mildly. "Do you ever imagine I would walk over you, Pierrot?"

Charity had not dared to meet his eyes. Astrea was ill

enough to be humored in her statements, it was clear, but she had no wish to be drawn into such meaningless personalities.

"Well, do you?" he persisted when she did not reply, but Astrea intervened.

"Ah, Pierrot . . ." she said, and began to sing in a wavering thread of the voice which had once been famous: "*Au clair de la lune . . . mon ami Pierrot* . . . She is like Pierrot, isn't she, Marc? You would have none of her then—or she of you . . . *Ma chandelle est morte* . . . That's true, too. My candle is burnt out . . . I had so much hoped that you and she—but no matter. I'm near the end, am I not, dear boy?"

He bent over to the bed. His face had changed as he listened to the cracked old voice trying to sing that familiar nursery song, and Charity saw a great tenderness there and a strange sort of hunger, as if he too could be moved by the simple things which brought tears.

"If you are, Astrea, you've had a good innings," he told her gently. "What is it you want of us?"

"I don't know . . . I don't know . . ." she answered fretfully. "If Roma hadn't come home . . . I don't know, Marc . . . but who will look after my little Ganymede now?"

"I've asked her to marry me. Wouldn't that do?" he said, and her old eyes lit up with a semblance of their remembered fire.

"Dear child . . ." she said, stretching out a hand to Charity. "Dear boy . . . can I die on that?"

"You are not going to die yet," Marc said, and frowned on Charity's instinctive recoil. "Would it make you happy if Charity would have me? She turned me down, you know."

"Turned you down? But perhaps she was thinking of Roma."

"Perhaps she was. Were you, Charity?"

Charity did not know where to look. Astrea was being

humored, she knew—she might even be dying—but it was
no reason for Marc to stand there on the other side of the
bed, looking at her with the old mockery, daring her
protest.

"It was all a hoax. He was making fun of me," she said
and saw the sudden glint in Marc's eyes. "Astrea—it's unfair to—to chivvy us both."

"Chivvy!" For a moment the voice was the remembered
one, the deep tones of outrage and personal affront. "I am
not aware that I have ever chivvied anyone into anything,
and my nephew, dear child, would scarcely choose that
method of making fun of you. Have you no fondness for
him?"

The last of the daylight seemed suddenly to fail and they
were, all three, dim, anonymous figures, grouped together
for one last question and answer. Even the birds had
stopped singing.

"I—I—" Charity stammered, unable to lie, but unable,
too, to confess her feelings under the cryptic regard of that
still figure the other side of the bed.

Astrea sank back on to her pillows and her breathing
became a little labored.

"Never mind," she said. "Give me your hands, both of
you." She took their outstretched hands, joining them
together across the bed, and Charity felt the cool, firm
touch of Marc's fingers on hers. "Now, you have pledged
your troth over what is, probably, my deathbed. You will
not go back on your word, my little Ganymede?"

It was, Charity knew, only one of the histrionic
moments in which Astrea so much delighted, it might even
be her last, but she could not resist saying with indignation, "I haven't given my word," and immediately felt
Marc's hard, unyielding grasp tighten on her hand.

"You have given it now," he said sternly. "Let truth
wait till another time."

"Truth?" said Astrea vaguely, but she began to wander. "Do you remember the fireworks in my honor?" she said. "And the time they took the horses out of the carriage . . . and the time the Crown Prince followed me to Ankara? . . . Ah, no, you were scarcely born . . ."

Minnie had come into the room and she went to straighten the worn tapestry which served as a cover.

"Yes, ducks," she said, relinquishing all the wordy arguments of other days. "He was incog. as you've always said, but he made you the toast of the town. Rest now, dearie. I'm going to draw the curtains."

Marc stooped over the bed to kiss his aunt.

"Goodnight," he said softly. "Are you content, now?"

Astrea only smiled and held out her hand to Charity.

"Goodnight, dear child," she murmured in a whisper. "Be good to Marc . . ."

They left the room together and, on the landing, Charity turned up her face to his.

"Is she going to die?" she asked solemnly, and felt his glance flick over her, cool, deliberate, and a little impersonal.

"Perhaps," he said. "Did you grudge making an old woman happy at the end?"

"Of course not, only—well, it was just make-believe, like the rest, wasn't it?"

In the darkness of the landing his face was unreadable, but his voice, when he replied, held the old note of mockery.

"It depends on what you designate as make-believe, Charity Child. For my own part, I'm not in the habit of jesting about things that matter. Goodnight—or are you coming downstairs for the rest of the evening?"

It was dismissal, and she was glad of it. She could not have borne to spend the rest of the evening with him. It must, she supposed vaguely, be long past the dinner hour, but let Roma and himself partake of the meal alone and make up their differences if they could. She bade him a brief goodnight and shut herself into her own room.

SHE SLEPT so heavily that she did not hear the disturbance during the night; the whispers and the running footsteps, the doctor's car arriving and leaving on the other side of the house. It was Minnie who, in the morning, told her that Astrea was dead, and stood there, twisting her old, work-roughened hands together in dumb acceptance.

At first Charity could not believe it. She had known that last attack to have been a grave one, but it was so typical of the old prima donna to have staged the sort of deathbed scene of the night before for her own amusement, that she could not rid herself of the notion that the whole thing was a hoax designed to embarrass them all. One look at Marc's face when they met for breakfast, however, told her the truth. He was freshly shaved, but his elegant clothes which needed pressing and the drawn look on his lean face gave evidence that he had been up most of the night.

"Why didn't you wake me?" she asked him over and over again. "Why didn't you call me when you knew?"

"Because she wouldn't have known you," he told her with unusual gentleness. "At the end it was only Roma she thought of. The rest was just a desire to lick old wounds, you know."

"The rest? You mean—" For a wild moment Charity had a vision of that same scene being enacted all over again, with Roma taking her place, her hand joined with Marc's over the bed.

"No," he said dryly, his shrewd glance testifying that once again he had read her thoughts. "I did not pledge myself to Roma to satisfy a dying woman. Astrea's desires had gone beyond that—back to her own youth, perhaps."

"Did she—did Roma—"

"Oh, yes. Roma behaved with propriety. She even managed to shed a tear."

"How bitter you sound!"

"Bitter!" His face was suddenly old and haggard. "Do you think it's pleasant to be reminded of one's own stupidity—to see people as they really are?"

Charity's less complex emotions could only place one construction on his outburst.

"You still love her," she said sadly, and his smile held tenderness and sudden compassion for her simplicity. Before he could answer her, however, Roma came into the room. It was evident that she still wore nothing under the long green housecoat which became her so well, but she had made up her face with her usual care.

"It was scarcely fitting to expect breakfast trays this morning, so I came down," she said. "Are you going to town, Marc?"

"Naturally not. I must stay to make the necessary arrangements."

"It's funny how funerals always come under that heading," she said, pouring heself some coffee. "You will get in touch with old Fenimore, too, I imagine. Do we have to wait for him to know what was in that will?"

"Oh, really, Roma!" Charity exclaimed, her voice sick with disgust.

"Come off it, honey!" retorted Roma, quite unmoved. "Don't *you* want to know where you stand?"

"No. I wish—I wish there had never been any question of a will at all, and if I *should* have been mentioned in it, then you can have my share."

Marc's eyes went curiously from one to the other of them. Beside Roma's vivid beauty, Charity looked washed out and insignificant.

"You don't need to worry, Charity, you don't benefit," he said, and Roma turned eyes brilliant with expectation upon him.

"Having gone so far you might as well tell us the rest," she said. "And I must say I'm surprised, since you drew the thing up, that you allowed your ewe lamb to be cut out."

"Are you, Roma? But, you see, Charity won't need the money. I have other plans for her."

Roma's eyes narrowed.

"Really?" she drawled. "And where do I come in—or don't I?"

"Oh, yes," he replied. "You come in, as you put it, just where you expected."

"Sole legatee?"

"Well, Minnie is provided for, naturally."

"Naturally, but that can't amount to much. What was the old girl worth, Marc?"

Charity wondered if she had only imagined the reservation in Marc's replies. She did not want to share in a discussion which now no longer concerned her, but she could not bear to leave him to the insensitive avidity of a girl for whom he might still cherish a stubborn fondness.

He stirred his coffee with deliberation before answering, swallowed a mouthful, then pushed it aside because it had grown cold. Charity automatically began to refill his cup.

"Astrea's affairs were not at all as we imagined them to be," he said then. "She was always very close, if you remember. I imagine old Fenimore was the only person who knew the truth."

"The truth?" Roma's eyes were suddenly hard and wary.

"Astrea has, apparently, been living on capital for years. These household economics she effected, her own personal expenditure, became necessary."

Charity, not as yet understanding, watched Roma's face whiten and grow suddenly older.

"But that's absurd!" she exclaimed. "Stubbs' sausages made mints—they still do."

Marc's smile was not pleasant to see.

"Oh, yes," he said. "Unfortunately for you, the firm passed into other hands after Stubbs died. Astrea sold out for a lump sum and the money was never properly invested, so you see, my dear Roma, although you are, in fact, the sole legatee after Minnie's legacy has been paid, there will be nothing worth calling an income, much less a fortune."

There was a brief, dreadful little silence, then Roma sprang to her feet, sweeping a whole collection of cutlery to the floor with the loose sleeve of her housecoat.

"You devil, Marc!" she cried. "You knew, and you've chosen to take your revenge this way! I hope you've enjoyed your charming little game with me."

"A, I knew nothing of my aunt's affairs until yesterday morning," he retorted, quite unmoved. "B, my intentions have never been dignifed by melodramatic thoughts of revenge, and C, I no longer play games with you, my dear; such pleasantries were finished with a long time ago."

To Charity he sounded cruel by very reason of his calmness, for he spoke with a dispassionate quiet that was more insulting than anger. She knew then that whatever her own doubts, Roma had no more power to hurt him, and because in a different measure, she too had been humiliated by him, she could feel it in her heart to pity Roma.

"Marc, please—" she protested, longing to get out of the room, but it was Roma who went.

"You're nothing but a cold, calculating legal machine with the dust of musty briefs, instead of blood, in your veins! I wish you joy of him, Charity, you poor simpleton!" she cried furiously, and slammed out of the dining room.

"Well," said Marc, not even turning his head as the door banged, "and do you consider that I have the dust of musty briefs in my veins instead of blood?"

She did not understand how much he had been holding himself in check, and could only marvel at his callousness. The humiliations she herself had suffered at his hands, and her own personal grief for Astrea, set a spark to her temper so that she turned on him unthinkingly.

"How can you behave like this with—with Astrea lying

dead upstairs?'' she demanded, and saw his eyebrows lift.

"Do the conventions demand hypocrisy of you, Charity? I had thought you more honest," he said.

His change of tone and expression should have warned her, but she was past caring what he thought of her.

"And *I* had thought you kinder, or at least more courteous," she retorted.

"I was not aware that I had been discourteous," he replied coldly. "As to kindness, you should not look for that where you least expect to find it."

She was aware, now, of the pinched look about his nostrils, of the taut restraint which she had mistaken for indifference. She was aware, too, that although he had held his temper in check without apparent difficulty with Roma, he was not prepared to afford her the same forbearance.

"I—I'm sorry," she stammered. "This must all have been a great strain for you. I—I'm apt to forget that Astrea was your aunt."

"You're apt to forget a good many things, aren't you?" he replied with dangerous calm. "Among them the fact that you gave your promise last night to a dying woman. I can see I shall have to take you in hand once we're married."

She stared at him stupidly, then the color rushed to her face.

"But that was a whim of Astrea's!" she exclaimed. "You would never hold me to that!"

"Why not? Weren't you serious?"

"As serious as you. I thought you understood."

"I understood very well, my dear. You had already turned me down. How else was I to get you to change your mind?"

He had risen to his feet and began to collect the morning papers and the little pile of bills and letters which had come for his aunt. He was, it was clear, prepared to leave her on this outrageous note of uncertainty.

"You—you *can't* be serious!" she exclaimed.

"Why not? You heard me tell Roma you wouldn't need the money as I had other plans for you."

"You have no right in any plans for my future," she said, and he smiled a little crookedly.

"Oh, yes, I think so. We've blown hot and cold too long, owing to one thing and another; it's time we came to an understanding," he said quite pleasantly, and left the room without another word.

The next few days had a dream-like quality for Charity in which more personal matters were lost. She scarcely saw Marc or Roma, for he was busy with his aunt's affairs and she hired the village car and went off on her own pursuits. When they all three met in the evenings they were studiously polite to one another, but by tacit consent they no longer used the music-room. Charity, left much to herself, wandered aimlessly round the house, wondering what would become of all the ill-assorted treasures Astrea had collected through the years. Few of them could be worth very much except to a collector of souvenirs, and Roma had made no secret of her intention to sell up Cleat House and its contents for the highest price everything would fetch.

"It seems sad to think of all these things going under the hammer," Charity said to Minnie. "Is there nothing you would like for yourself to remind you of her? I'm sure Miss Roma would understand."

"Miss Roma don't care one way or the other so long as she gets the cash," Minnie replied, and Charity looked shocked.

"But she wouldn't *sell* you mementoes of Madam!" she exclaimed, but the old dresser's wrinkled face creased in a sour smile.

"Maybe not," she said, "but I prefer to buy and take my pick, young miss. I'll not be beholden, no more than you."

"What will you do, Minnie?" It was hard to say how deeply affected she had been by Astrea's death, but her future often worried Charity.

"Go back to the North End Road where I come from. The liver and lights shop is still there."

"The liver and lights shop?" Charity frowned, trying to remember where she had heard the phrase before.

"The start of Stubbs' sausages—didn't Madam ever tell you?"

"Oh, of course! But what had it to do with you?"

"My dad worked there with Stubbs' governor—back in '98 that was. When Albert, the son, started his sausage factories, the shop passed to Dad. Funny, isn't it, how our paths crossed? M'lady, of course, said it was all written in the stars, which sounded a mort of nonsense to me, though it was through me, mark you, that she ran across Albert Stubbs in the end. You didn't know that, did you?"

"No," said Charity, marvelling at this strange glimpse of old history. "Who owns the shop now?"

"Cousin by marriage of me dad's. She's widowed now, but she used to dress the chorus at the old Paladrome in years gone by—bit different to Madam's classy turn-out, but all in the same business, so to speak. I'll put the bit of money Madam's left me in with her and she'll be a nice bit of company."

A reminiscent and slightly roguish gleam had come into the old dresser's round bright eyes, and Charity could suddenly see her for what she once must have been, a gay and rather tough young Cockney, sacrificing the pleasures of quite a different environment in order to better herself and, in the end, sink her individuality in the nebulous rôle of housekeeper.

"How little one knows people," she said, and thought, for almost the first time since Astrea's death, with serious deliberation of Marc. Was he too another person under that studied façade he liked people to believe was himself? Did they all show a different front to the curious eyes of the world; Astrea with her histrionics, Marc with his fastidious mockery, Roma with her worldly hardness? And what of Charity Child, she thought humbly; did she show only pride and rejection because she so passionately desired the opposite and was afraid of being laughed at?

Minnie was watching her with a suddenly knowing look.

"We must know ourselves, young miss, before we can know others," she said.

"Yes. How wise you are." For some unexplained reason, Charity suddenly stooped and kissed the old woman, and Minnie pushed her away with a cluck of impatience.

"Oh, get away with you! You're soft-spoken, even to the likes of me, and that's in your favor, but go out for what you want, ducks—don't let 'em walk on you! I've no patience with the shilly-shallying kind, and neither had Madam." Minnie spoke sharply, with her old lack of forbearance at the many changes she had seen at Cleat, but her eyes held a sudden, surprising moisture.

"Will you be happy in the shop in the North End Road?" asked Charity anxiously, because the breakup of Cleat, although she had been there such a short time, seemed suddenly to matter very much.

"Happiness is where you find it. Don't you know that yet, young miss?" retorted Minnie, and went back to her kitchen where the daily women were waiting to afford her the respectful but enjoyable attentions due to the bereaved.

ON THE day of the funeral, villagers climbed Cleat Hill to lay flowers on the porch. Astrea had known none of them intimately, but she was, nevertheless, the district's celebrity. She would be buried in Cleat churchyard, and for ever afterwards her grave would be pointed out to tourists and her memory kept green.

To Charity, the small offerings were infinitely pathetic; little bunches of primroses, almost over, daffodils which had bloomed their best before April was out, and the first early roses from cottage gardens. But there were wreaths, too, opulent beside the humbler offerings; lilies, carnations, even orchids, tributes from the few professionals who remembered Astrea and had read her small obituary in *The Times*. There were few mourners to follow the coffin and the service was short and simple. As she heard the bell toll on that sunny afternoon in May, Charity's thoughts turned to Housman and she wondered if Marc too was remembering. *They tolled the one bell only . . . and so to church went she . . .*

Quite suddenly she understood him. His obsession with Housman was a clear pointer, for was it not a philosophy shared because life had taught him, too young, to accept the things that came too late? Was he not as simple as she, desiring still the goodness and felicity of what had been denied him earlier? She looked at his straight back as he stood, rigid and erect beside Roma in the pew in front, and her love flowed out to him, a love for her father's companionship had made possible for a man so much older than herself. In Astrea's passing there was now no great sorrow, for she had come to rest, but, dwelling on this small, insignificant last gathering, Charity knew a moment's affectionate sympathy for that out-dated spirit. How Astrea would have enjoyed the grave panoply of plumed black horses and sable trappings, the funeral orations of bygone years; just so should Astrea, the Star-maiden, the toast of a more colorful era, have gone to her final rest.

"Are you all right?" she heard Marc whisper as they began to file out of the little church, and she realized she must look strange, still locked in the absurd realms of her imagination.

"Quite all right," she told him with a smile. "I was just thinking of the horses and their plumes."

His eyebrows rose a fraction with quizzical enquiry, then he smiled.

"I see what you mean," he murmured, and they came out to the sunlit peace of the little country churchyard with the clear sky arched above them and the blue curve of the downs beyond. Charity's eyes went instinctively to the long ridge which was Cleat Beacon, and Marc's gaze followed.

"Later?" he said. She did not answer, but moved on to the graveside to stand beside old Minnie for the final commitment to earth.

Roma stood beside Marc, beautiful and unmoved by the curious glances of the villagers, her face a mask of hardness. In the sunlight her hair shone like a burnished aureole, just as Astrea's must once have done.

Marc drove them all back to Cleat House, empty and indifferent in its mock-Gothic ugliness, and Roma went upstairs to pack. She was, she had announced earlier, removing herself to London as soon as the funeral was over; she could not endure much more of rustic stagnation.

Charity went to her room to change into slacks. She would go the Beacon, and whether Marc came to find her there or not did not really matter. On Cleat Beacon she had been made aware of many things which, as yet, life had not begun to teach her; there she would bring order to her thoughts and learn to face the future.

Climbing the chalk track which had so often before led his steps to the crest of the Beacon, Marc saw her outlined against the sky. The wind lashed the black, tapered slacks against her long legs and the hair from her eyes; her face was lifted to the breeze, and her slender body seemed caught for a moment in a familiar drooping curve. She was as he always thought of her, the sad pierrot of tradition, lost and forlorn because nowhere had she found to lay her head and heart.

"Well—" he said as he walked along the ridge to meet her. "Are you waiting for me, or do I turn back?"

The smile she gave him was questioning and a little remote. She could not, as yet, read what was written for her in his face, and she was, for perhaps the last time, still a little unsure of him.

"Did you remember in church about the one bell tolling?" she asked, and he smiled.

"*Summer time on Bredon?* Yes, but Housman also had a happier one.

> '*And now the fancy passes by,*
> *And nothing will remain,*
> *And miles around they'll say that I*
> *Am quite myself again*'."

"But that," she said quickly, "was a rather cynical postscript to the first verse."

"So it was," he replied with a wry smile. "I must remember in future that you are too familiar with our mutual friend to quote out of context."

"He's made me understand you a little," she said shyly.

"Has he? Well, at your age you shouldn't care for such a philosophy. I'm not sure I always do, myself. Let's walk." He took her arm and began to march her along the ridge of the Beacon towards the chalk hollow in the breast of downland where they had sheltered that rainy afternoon and he had called her a scarecrow.

She looked about her, aware of changes everywhere. Speedwell and pimpernel showed among the tufty grass, the lambs had grown big and lost their grace, and the dewponds, filled with spring rain, presented clear mirrors to the sky.

"How lovely it all is," she said with faint regret. "How strange that life should go on, no matter what happens."

"Not strange—only natural," he said. "Does Astrea's death matter so much to you?"

"Yes, in a way. Cleat was the first real home I'd had since my father died."

They had reached the hollow, and he drew her down into it out of the wind and the bare exposure of the downs.

"Well," he said, "you have your remedy. I can offer you a home, even if nothing else appeals."

She turned to look at him, startled by the sudden humility in his voice, and saw the mixture of purpose and uncertainty in his face.

"Would you be willing to offer me a home, and nothing more?" she asked wonderingly.

"If necessary—though I would hope for something better in the end. Could you not give me that expectation, do you think?"

She was so close to him that she could see the small, puckered lines of anxiety at the corners of his mouth, and the urgent question in his eyes. It was so strange to see him humble and uncertain that she could find no words to reassure him, for had it not been he who had always called the tune and made of her what he would?

"Oh, Marc . . ." she said, and her eyes filled with tears.

He stretched tentative hands towards her, touching her lightly, with no hint of the possession he had shown once before.

"I love you very much, Pierrot," he told her gravely. "So much that if you'll still have none of me I'll leave you and wish you well."

The tears flowed over then, and her hands went to meet his, her fingers entwining, bringing the comfort which she now knew he asked of her.

"That I couldn't bear," she said, "for if you left me now, I would have nothing. Were you—were you not making fun of me, after all?"

He pulled her into his arms and his cheek was rough against hers.

"I never made fun of you, my darling," he said. "I was clumsy and out of tune with the moment that day. You were, you see, so young, so inexperienced, and were raising such valiant barriers of pride between us. Have you not heard the trumpets yet?"

"The trumpets?"

"Don't you remember? 'When the people heard the sound of the trumpet . . . the wall fell flat . . .' That's what you were thinking when we drove back to Cleat that day, wasn't it?"

"Yes, and you knew. You always do know what I'm thinking, Marc, it's—it's most disconcerting."

His eyes were suddenly grave and searching and the little nerve in his cheek betrayed his own uncertainty.

"Not always," he said. "I was never sure if you could love me. I'm not sure yet."

"Aren't you, Marc?" she whispered. "Haven't you always known that I wouldn't be proof against you? I have no experience of men like you—nor indeed of any man, except my father."

His expression was wryly tender.

"And you still want to put me in his place?"

"No," she said on a long sigh. "I want you for what you are and for what I can give you, if you'll let me and—and—I don't feel at all like a daughter to you."

"I should hope not!" he retorted with something of his old assurance, then, before he kissed her, he took her face between his two hands searching it hungrily for the qualities he would always remember; the grave, enquiring eyes, the plaintive brows, the innocent, generous promise of the young, untutored mouth.

"You have all the advantages over me, after all, Charity Child," he said softly, and found her mouth with his.

Just what the woman on the go needs!

BOOK MATE

The perfect "mate" for all Harlequin paperbacks

Traveling • Vacationing • At Work • In Bed • Studying • Cooking • Eating

Perfect size for all standard paperbacks, this wonderful invention makes reading a pure pleasure! Ingenious design holds paperback books OPEN and FLAT so even wind can't ruffle pages — leaves your hands free to do other things. Reinforced, wipe-clean vinyl-covered holder flexes to let you turn pages without undoing the strap...supports paperbacks so well, they have the strength of hardcovers!

Pages turn WITHOUT opening the strap.

"CLICK"

SEE-THROUGH STRAP

Reinforced back stays flat.

Built in bookmark.

BOOK MARK

BACK COVER HOLDING STRIP

10" x 7¼", opened.
Snaps closed for easy carrying, too.